TAKE NOTE!

By

Gill Burnett

DEDICATION

For my Mam and Dad.

CONTENTS

'I do not like money. Money is the reason we fight!'

- Karl Marx

The good old British £10 note is familiar to all of us. For some, they have them in abundance; small change, you might say. For others they are Scotch mist, rarely seen and hard to keep hold of. But what is a £10 note worth? Is there really a value to it?

This is the story of a plain old £10 note. Exactly the same as any £10 note that you have in your possession now. Brown in colour, depicting Charles Darwin on the back and Queen Elizabeth II on the front. But each one is unique. If you look closely on the front of the note you will see horizontally in the top left-hand corner and again vertically down the right there is a number.

This £10 note, whose story you are about to read, is HE75 229564. It's one of a kind. It travels its own journey, telling its own tale. There won't be another £10 note that will travel the same route.

What is a £10 note worth? Or more to the point, how much is HE75 229564 worth?

1

You Can't Take It With You

Rita Simms put on her shoes and coat, picked up her purse and her shopping bag and made for the door. It was Tuesday and every Tuesday she made the same journey. She left the house at 8.30, or thereabouts, and took the 15-minute walk to the Post Office. It was a 15-minute walk, but that was two years ago, now it took her more like 25 minutes, sometimes longer. There were times when she had to step up the pace; she hated being late and having to join the queue that ran outside the door, especially in the winter, it was just too cold to be standing around waiting for the queue to go down enough so she could get into the shop. Even then, the door was often propped open and the cold wind would blow and chill her bones. On those days it would take the walk home, a pot of tea and a sit for an hour in front of two bars on her electric fire to thaw her through. So she always tried to give herself enough time so at least she was somewhere near the front of the queue, protected by the elements in the huddle of the other pensioners.

Tuesday was pension day. For years her pension had been paid into her bank account, but she didn't like it. She didn't trust banks, so that was the reason she made the trek to the Post Office, to take the money out that had been deposited in her bank account earlier that day. But she didn't like going. At one time her Post Office branch had just been around the corner, but it wasn't cost effective to run it, so like everything else in her area, it was closed down and boarded up. She liked her old Post Office. Mrs Bradford, the Post Mistress, had run it for years. She knew everyone that went into her shop, knew them and knew their families. She was part of the community.

Now there wasn't any community. Rita's neighbours had all long gone; died; moved into sheltered accommodation, or just moved out of the area. The once pristine street where everyone took pride in their little terraced houses, was now shabby and run down. The street was scattered with boarded-up houses; apart from one or two people, Rita knew no one. But it was the house she had lived in for all her married life and she wasn't going anywhere else anytime soon, no matter how run down and dated it was.

Closing the front door behind her and giving the customary push against it to make sure it was locked, Rita set off. Even though the street wasn't anywhere near the street she had moved into all those years earlier, she still loved it. It reminded her of herself. She had been a blushing bride, all legs and good looks when Billy had carried her across the threshold. What dreams they had had. They were going to live in the little two-up, two-down for a few years, save up and then move into one of the new semi-detached houses they were building on the outskirts of the town. But it hadn't happened and to be honest, Rita wasn't bothered; she loved that house and she couldn't imagine living anywhere else. Even when the kids had come along and the house had been cram-packed, it had been home and they had been happy there.

But one by one each of her five children had left home and when Billy had died just before his 55th birthday, the house seemed huge and she would find herself rattling around it. Now it seemed even bigger to her; she struggled to keep up with the housework and the inside of the house was beginning to look as shabby as the outside. Luckily, the bathroom was in the little extension at the back of the kitchen so even though her children had clubbed together to have her a stairlift fitted, she rarely went upstairs now.

Leaving her street behind her, she continued along the terraces, passing children on their way to school. How many times had she made this journey herself? It didn't bear thinking about; she had had five children in under eight years. For that time she felt like she was continually pregnant or pushing a pram. She could remember her mam having a go at her for not being more careful; no sooner was there a baby in the pram then there would be another on the way. She loved Billy and just couldn't say no. But after the fifth they were more careful; they just couldn't afford another mouth to feed and luckily it hadn't happened.

Rita took pride in her kids; they were clean, well fed and cared for. She hadn't been able to go back to work until the youngest was at school full-time, but she had been a canny manager, mainly thanks to her own mam who had brought up 11 children virtually on thin air. Her own children were all wanted and loved. By her and Billy. In the days when men were men and didn't show their feelings much, Billy lavished each of the kids in time and love, even after he came in after a 12-hour shift. He had time for them all.

So she couldn't complain, she had had a happy marriage. Her children all had children of their own now and even some of them were starting to have kids. She was a great-grandmother. Her little living room was testament of her ever increasing family; there were photographs everywhere. She loved to look at them all, look for resemblances, but they were a bind too – it took her forever to dust them all. Her memory not being what it used to be, she had to write all the names down, especially her grandchildren and their other halves, they seemed to change so often. But she made sure that whenever there was a new addition or a change of partner she wrote it down, she would hate to get it wrong.

It was the same with her diary; every year she would transfer the birthdays into the next year's carefully. It was a huge task and one she started as soon as she bought her new diary at the Post Office before the end of the year was even out. But there were just so many of them, she couldn't begin to remember them all. It seemed that every week she had to buy a card for someone. Today it was for granddaughter Kate; she would be turning 21 at the end of the week so Rita would have to buy a card and stamp today and then maybe if she was feeling up to it, she would take it to the post box around the corner from her house this afternoon. She would rather it arrived early, even posting it first-class didn't guarantee next-day delivery these days and she would hate for it to be late.

The weather wasn't so bad and she was enjoying her walk. The cobwebs were beginning to blow away and the bite that had been in the air the previous week wasn't there, and she could step out a little bit without losing her breath. She liked to walk; always had. Billy had been the driver in the house; driving a car was something she hadn't even considered. What would she want driving a car when she had two perfectly good feet? But having a car had been nice. They had saved and saved to buy their first car and it had been Billy's pride and joy. She had sometimes thought he had loved that car more than her. But it was long gone, just like Billy, and her feet and her bus pass had served her well enough since then.

The walk always made her think about the past. Maybe it was the places she passed on the way. The church where she and Billy had married, the kids had been christened, two of her three daughters had been married and of course where they had held Billy's funeral. Bittersweet memories, but memories nonetheless. She always meant to take the short walk to church on a Sunday morning, she would like to go, but Sunday would arrive and by the time she had got herself dressed, had her breakfast and done her few chores, it would be too late and she would chide herself for being so tardy with her time and vow to herself that she would go next week. But of course next week never came.

Then she would pass the school where all her

children had attended. It wasn't a school anymore, it was some kind of nursery. She would see the mams and dads rushing in with their little ones on their way to work. Some of them were just babies!! Times had changed; in her day most mams didn't go to work and they certainly didn't have the luxury of a nursery to leave their little ones at. If Rita had wanted to do anything she would leave her kids in the capable hands of Mrs Allen next door; and she would do the same. That was the way it was.

Poor Mrs Allen, Rita thought. They had been neighbours for over 40 years; 10 of those years they had both been widows. But where she had just got on with it, Mrs Allen had taken widowhood badly. Rita had tried to keep an eye on her, but it had got to the point where Mrs Allen wouldn't let anyone into the house. Her daughter, Carol, turned up every other day with shopping and stuff, but the situation was getting out of hand. If anyone came to the door, Mrs Allen would shout and scream through the letterbox. It was pointless trying to talk to her, so Rita would pick up the telephone and call Carol or her other daughter, Susan, and one of them would call around and calm her down.

Dementia was mentioned; or was it Alzheimer's? Rita wasn't sure and really didn't know the difference, but either way the decision was made that Mrs Allen wasn't safe to be left on her own, a care home was found and the house went up onto the market. It was now owned by some property company and rented out. There always seemed to be a removal van at the door and she couldn't even think who lived there now. Mrs Allen had died a couple of years earlier. Rita had gone to her funeral, how could she not? They had been friends and neighbours for so long. She had fond memories of her neighbour and some not so fond; times had been hard sometimes for both of them. But she missed her, she liked the comfort of knowing who she was living next door to.

It was the same on the other side. A lady called Erica lived there now with her teenage daughter whose name she couldn't remember. But before that Sally and Tom had lived there. They hadn't lived there as long as Mrs Allen, maybe 20 years, and it was always strange to be on first-name terms with them. But they were younger and wouldn't hear of themselves being called Mr and Mrs Ball, likewise they called her Rita, no Mrs Simms for them or their children. They had been a nice family though, nothing was ever too much trouble for them and they always kept an eye out for her. But they had moved on too. When their only child had grown up and settled himself 200 miles away, they had sold their house and bought one nearer to him and his small family. Rita still got a Christmas card off them every year though, and a note enquiring about her health and that of her family. They were a miss.

Rita turned into the little parade of shops, her destination in sight. It was 8.50 and she had made good time. She couldn't see a queue forming outside the door so maybe she would be able to stand the last few minutes before the Post Office opening in the relative warmth of the shop.

Years ago, this little parade of shops was where you came for your shopping. It had everything you would need. To the left there had been a Co-op which sold everything from socks and shoes to groceries and it even sold furniture. It was the place you went to first for anything you wanted. Opposite there had been an array of other shops. A little ladieswear shop which also sold wool and material, a wet fish shop, a butchers, a bakers, no candlestick maker, but there was a hardware shop that sold candles; obviously they had been made by someone else.

The parade had been thriving. It wasn't thriving now. The Co-op had long closed its doors; it had been converted into plush flats and on the opposite side there were none of the original shops left. Even the old Post Office had gone. It had been one of the bigger ones that acted as a sorting office, but it had become surplus to requirements and they had moved the Post Office counter into one of the 'Open All Hours' convenience shops that had taken up residence in the old DIY shop.

It was all change all of the time. As Rita made her way up to the last shop, she passed the bookies, thrift shop, hairdressers and one of the sunbed thing shops. There was nothing practical there; it was a good job the Post Office shop sold everything she needed. Once a month her eldest daughter, Christine, would come and collect her and take her to the big supermarket on the edge of town where she could buy everything in one go. It was her favourite day. Even if she couldn't be bothered she wouldn't not go. She would force herself around the huge shop, pushing her trolley.

As careful as ever, she would always have a list with her and she would stick to it. Impulse buying had never been a luxury she could afford and it was something she wasn't taking up in her old age. But she would write the odd treat on her list or something she needed like some new bedding, that way she could justify putting it into her trolley. Christine always tried to get her to buy a lovely cardigan or a skirt or something, but if she didn't need it she wasn't buying it. But even when she stuck to her list, the trolley would be jam-packed and Christine would have a job filling the bags as it all went through the check-out.

So usually on a Tuesday she would just pick up a few fresh things; a bit of fruit or a packet of ham, sometimes something nice for her tea.

By the time she got into the shop there were three in the queue in front of her. All pensioners like herself. Even though the queue was short, she would still be waiting her turn for a while. It was the chip and pin thing that slowed them all down. She wasn't comfortable doing it herself and always seemed to put the card in the wrong way around, or she pressed the buttons too fast and the whole transaction would have to start again.

But she was patient. Her turn would probably take a bit longer than most, she needed stamps and she had a few bills to pay and TV Licence stamps to buy; so she would wait. There would be no sighing or tutting or stamping feet from Rita Simms, it wasn't her style. And soon enough it was her turn. She didn't recognise the Post Mistress, another new one, but she seemed pleasant enough and for once she managed to get the card in the right way and her fingers hit all the buttons in a timely manner. Job done, she thanked the young lady and made her way over to where the greeting cards were stocked.

She only needed one birthday card this week, but she wanted a nice one for Kate; it was her 21st and that warranted a special card. She took her time, there was nothing for her to rush around for now she had her pension safely tucked into her purse and the few things she needed to pay had been sorted. For a little shop they had a good selection and there were one or two that caught her eye. In the end it was down to the verse on the inside of the card. Nothing too slushy, but indicating that she would be thinking about her on her special day.

Picking up a basket, she placed the card in the bottom and then made her way around the little shop. Ten minutes later she was out of the door, her shopping bag overfilled considering she now had to carry it all of the way home, but she would take her time. There was a weak sun shining so she would make the most of it and amble home.

More thinking time. It was funny because even though she was on her own most of the time, her little walks on a Tuesday were the time when all her thoughts and worries of the week would come to the fore. Not that she had a lot to worry about, she had a roof over her head, food in her cupboard and a little bit of money in her purse. But she worried about her family. They never came to her with their concerns, but she knew of old that sometimes a comment made over the telephone veiled something bigger. And it was on these walks where the worries would pop into her head.

Take Christine. She had rung on Sunday night as she was in the habit of doing. She called on a Friday night on her way home from work and then would telephone on a Sunday and Wednesday. She was Rita's eldest, married to Bob. They had had three children – Liam, Niall and Kate. All three were still living at home even though Liam was now in his mid-20s and Kate was turning 21. But Christine was worried about Kate; she could hear the concern in her voice when Rita had asked if they were doing anything special for Kate's birthday. No, Kate was going out with her friends. This baffled Rita. Kate was their baby, but not only that, they had always celebrated each birthday as a family. Sometimes they had asked her to go along, but it was usually on a night and Rita didn't like going back into an empty house on a night-time. But the lack of celebration for Kate made her think that there was more to it than met the eye. It was a worry.

It was shopping week next week, maybe Christine would shed a bit more light onto it then.

She was nearing home; she had enjoyed her walk. Her arm was aching carrying her shopping bag, but she would be home soon and she would be able to put her feet up with a cup of milky coffee. Hopefully she would be able to catch the end of the property programme she was fond of watching every morning. It always surprised her what you could do if you had a bit of money. Her house always looked dated in comparison, but it didn't bother her; it was her home.

Letting herself in, she took off her coat and shoes, put on her slippers and made her way to the little kitchen at the back of the house and put away the bits of shopping she had bought. She boiled some milk and added it to the coffee she had already put into her mug. She had treated herself to a nice peach melba, so taking them both into the living room, she put on the television and for the next half an hour was engrossed in her programme.

As it ended, she looked around her living room. It was cram-packed full of stuff; furniture, ornaments, photographs, basically her life. Even if someone came in and said that they would re-vamp it, she would probably refuse. It had been like this for so long it was like her comfort blanket. In fact her blankets and quilt were folded neatly at the end of the settee; she had stopped sleeping in her bed about six months ago. At first she had stayed downstairs because she hadn't been well and didn't want to have to go up and down the stairs to the loo; the stairlift was so slow and she was sure she would have an 'accident' on it on the way down. So she had bundled her quilt and pillows and had slept on the settee. One night had become two and then it was every night. She liked it; she would watch something on the telly until her eyes started to drop and then quickly switch the telly off, before she woke up properly again. She slept better and there was the added bonus that if she did need the loo she as only a few steps away from it. And of course she was right next to the kitchen. The nights that she woke at 2.30 and no matter how hard she tried couldn't get back to sleep, now she would get up, make herself a cup of tea and then snuggle back down under her sheets and quilt sipping on her tea and watching some rubbish on the telly. Many a time she would wake in the morning to find the lights still on and the telly blaring away to itself.

The family would go mad. So if any of them were

due she would hide the bedding away and say nothing about her sleeping arrangements. She didn't want them to think that she couldn't manage. The thought of having to leave her house filled her with dread and she was determined when she did leave, it would be in a wooden box.

Thinking of boxes, she got herself up out of her chair, took her dishes into the kitchen and picked up her purse. As she did every Tuesday, she went back into the living room, took out the two wooden boxes from the sideboard and went and sat down at the dining room table. She took what was left out of her pension money and divided it into little piles on the table. She still had the milkman to pay and it was window cleaner week, then there was the money she would need to put into Kate's card. The everyday money went into one box and the lid was put back on and the rest would go into the other. Opening the lid, she took out the loose notes and counted them – £80. She added another £20 out of her pension, rolled them up and then secured the roll with an elastic band. Dropping it inside the box she noted that there were quite a few bundles in there now; at least 20. The rest of her pension she put loosely in the box, replaced the lid and then carried both the boxes back to the sideboard.

Kate's card was on the sideboard so she picked it up along with her diary out of the drawer and made her way back to the dining room table. It really was a nice card and she hoped that Kate would like it. Normally she would have put £21 in the card, but she wouldn't be seeing Christine before Kate's birthday so she would be posting it. She didn't want anyone knowing there was money in the card and a £1 coin would certainly give the game away. So she was giving her £30; the crispy £20 and £10 notes were lying on the table ready.

A long time ago someone had told her if she was sending anything in the post then she must write the serial numbers of the money down. There were some unscrupulous people out there and if anything untoward did happen, then it would be a great help if she could give as much detail to the police as possible. So every time she sent a note off in the post, she wrote the serial numbers of the notes next to the recipient's name in her diary. She duly did that now: £20 – CE53 571204, £10 – HE75 229564.

Happy she had written the numbers down correctly, she signed the card, put in the money and sealed it. After addressing it and sticking the stamp on she looked out of the window. The sun continued to cast a bright light on the day, so she decided to put her shoes and coat on and go and post it now before the lunchtime news started, which she always liked to watch.

Out of her door, card in hand, she did her customary push against the door and went off up the street in the opposite direction to the one she had taken earlier that morning. Bathed in sunlight, the street didn't look so run down and shabby. The boarded-up houses were still boarded up, but the metal shutters twinkled in the sunlight. *The memories I have of this street!* she thought to herself.

By the time she arrived at the post box she was having a little argument with herself. Was £30 too much money? After all, the others hadn't had that much. But the things that Christine hadn't said were in the back of her mind. If there was trouble then maybe the £30 would help. She pushed the card into the box. It was done now, nothing she could do about it. Turning back towards home, she smiled. *After all, I can't take it with me, can I?*

2

The Penny Drops

Kate Lockey sat in the living room surrounded by cards and presents. It was her 21st birthday and looking around her, she knew she had been spoilt rotten as always, probably more so. Her mam and dad were with her, and her brothers. It was a tradition in their family. The present opening didn't begin until all five of them were together.

Her mam had been a bit 'off' with her for weeks. She had wanted them all to go out and celebrate together; just the five of them. Which meant that Kate's boyfriend of three years, Adam, wasn't invited. She was having none of it; if Adam couldn't go, then she wasn't going either. They were together and no matter what her mam and dad thought of him, if they wouldn't accept him, then the celebrations weren't happening.

But sitting in the midst of her family she felt bad. They had all gone to so much trouble for her special day. Adam so far hadn't even texted to say happy birthday never mind bought her a present, but the day was still young and she was sure that he wouldn't let her down. She intended to enjoy her birthday, with or without her family or Adam. At the minute she was happy to be opening her cards and presents and having a leisurely morning with her mam and dad.

Kate was right to think she had been spoilt, she had been. Perfume, make-up, jewellery, little silver bracelet from her brother Liam and a matching necklace from her other brother Niall. There were vouchers for makeovers and another voucher for Ticketmaster so she could put it towards seeing one of her favourite groups or singers. She had done really well. Piling the presents up, she made a start on her cards. There were so many of them, it seemed all of the family had remembered. She recognised her Nana Rita's handwriting straightaway. A pang of guilt sprang up. She kept promising herself that she would call and see her more, after all she drove now and it was only a 30-minute drive to her nana's house, but she hadn't and the months were passing by. The longer she left it the harder it would be; maybe she would go and see her with her mam next week.

More guilt when she opened the card. Not only was the card beautiful, but cash fell out of it onto her lap – £30. Her nana couldn't afford that; she had loads of grandchildren and a sprinkling of great-grandchildren, surely she couldn't put that amount of money into all the cards. Or was it because it was her 21st? She couldn't remember how much she had got last year, but was sure it wasn't that much. She really needed to go and see her. Her mam said Nana Rita was in good health but she was knocking towards 80; time wasn't a luxury for her. Picking a phone up and ringing her was something that didn't even cross through her head.

By the time she got to the bottom of the pile of cards, Nana Rita was forgotten. Not only did she have a huge pile of presents, she now had a huge pile of cash; at least £250. It was a happy Kate who made her way upstairs to shower, put on her clothes and check her mobile for a text from Adam. Of course there wasn't one. He had been out the night before so no doubt he hadn't surfaced out of his bed yet. But there were lots of other texts from friends and her Facebook page was amass with good wishes.

But as she stood under the shower ten minutes later, she wasn't happy. For once, why couldn't Adam have just put her first? Disappointed more than mad, she wasn't going to let Adam Mitchell spoil her day. Her family were downstairs waiting to have a champagne breakfast with her, she wasn't going to ruin it for them by having a miserable face. But her disappointment was there; it was a knot in her chest and she knew from experience that until Adam got in touch, it would remain there.

They had arranged to meet later for drinks with some friends; surely he would be in touch sometime in the next few hours. She wasn't going to ring him, this was what he did all of the time. A night out with his mates and Kate would be forgotten. She had lost count of the number of times he had let her down. But today was her 21st, surely he would make a bit of an effort!

She enjoyed her birthday breakfast. Her mam had gone to so much effort and it was nice that they all had the chance to sit around the dining room table, catch up and celebrate. Adam wasn't mentioned. Had her mam warned them all not to mention his name? *Probably!* she thought. She didn't mention him either, he was like a red rag to a bull as far as her mam was concerned. Christine just didn't like him and the more she said this to Kate, the more she dug her heels in and stuck up for him. So Adam was the elephant in the room. A taboo subject for that day at least; and at that time an ever elusive boyfriend.

By the time they had finished the birthday breakfast and washed up, it was almost lunch time. Liam and Niall were off out to the match. She kissed and cuddled them both before they went, thanking them for their gifts. As big brothers went they were okay. She would always be their baby sister and they would still treat her like a little girl, but she had a good relationship with both of them. Adam was Niall's friend and that was how Kate had met him. Her mam had never forgiven Niall for encouraging the relationship, but she wasn't stupid. If she was honest she would agree with her mam; Adam Mitchell was a handful.

She had met him three years ago at Niall's 21st birthday party. Adam was a college friend and had arrived in the middle of the night a bit worse for wear, but Kate thought he was the most beautiful boy she had ever seen. Shocked when he asked her to dance, she was as proud as punch when he led her onto the dancefloor and stayed there with her for the rest of the night. Niall had warned her before they had even left the party that Adam had a girlfriend, but she didn't care. All she had done was dance with him and if truth be known she knew he was out of her league. But it was something to tell her friends in sixth form the following Monday morning.

But before she even got to school on the Monday morning, Adam had found her on Facebook and they had exchanged numbers. Instinctively she knew she had to keep her budding friendship with Adam a secret; girls talked and she didn't want word getting back to his girlfriend. The thought of some girl turning up at the school gates and hitting her made her feel ill.

So in the beginning Kate and Adam's relationship was a secret. He was funny and clever and she loved every minute she spent with him. But then he would disappear, he wouldn't ring or text and she daren't try and find him; she didn't know who he was with or where he was at!! The only thing she could do was wait for him to get back in touch, but the whole Adam thing was having an effect on her life. She dropped nights out with her friends on the off chance he would call and want to see her. Which he eventually did. There would be no explanation to where he had been, he would just waltz back into her life and she would be grateful…

Adam left college and Kate left sixth form. Whereas she found a full-time job, Adam wasn't even looking. He spent his days with friends, or in the pub or at the bookies. When photographs appeared on Facebook of him snogging the face off some girl when he was on a night out, Kate was devastated, Adam's girlfriend more so, and he was dumped. The coast now clear for them to be together, they went public and Kate swallowed the story about the girl in the photographs being deliberate so his girlfriend Jo would dump him and he could be with her.

Kate and Adam became a couple. If her mam and dad weren't happy they didn't say anything. But she wasn't stupid, she knew Niall had been given the third degree from her mam and she knew they didn't think he was good enough for her. Like any savvy parent though, her mam had kept quiet; the last thing she wanted was for her 18-year-old daughter to up sticks and go and move in with her boyfriend because her parents didn't approve. So her mam had kept mum and made Adam welcome.

They had a turbulent relationship, more on Adam's part than hers; he would often not turn up when they arranged to do something. Kate was used to it and to the excuses he always had ready when he next got in contact. With still no sign of a job, he would often do an odd day's work for a bloke he knew; cash in hand, of course. He would work, get paid and then go on a bender with his mates. The thought of treating Kate was never an option.

But Kate adored him. When they were together he made her feel like she was the only girl in the whole wide world. He lavished her with affection and when they went out together anywhere he only had eyes for her. He was just so handsome and Kate often thought that her mam was wrong; she wasn't good enough for him!

The girls she worked with at the nursery all seemed to know Adam. It seemed he had a bit of a reputation for partying around town and they often broke their necks to tell her that they had seen him out on the previous Friday or Saturday night. She tended to not say anything to the girls about her plans; more often than not Adam wouldn't turn up and the first time she had said they were going to the pictures on the Friday night and he hadn't shown up, one of the girls deliberately made a show of Kate by saying she had seen him in the pub. She knew she would just keep quiet in future.

She liked her job though, she loved the children, especially the toddlers whose room she usually worked in. They were all just so funny. The girls she worked with were a mixed bag, some she had known before she got the job from school and college, and others she had just met there. Mostly they were all right, but one or two of them were just so full of themselves and she sometimes wondered how they had even managed to get the job.

There were a couple in particular who were proper party girls; they worked to play and every weekend they would be out partying, turning back up to work on a Monday morning looking like death. A far cry from the photographs that they constantly posted on Facebook where they were all hair extensions, an inch of make-up and short dresses. The two different versions were unrecognisable. And of course they knew Adam, so Kate was always on edge in case they carried tales about him into work. She just didn't want to know what him and his mates got up to. Like the two versions of the girls, there were two versions of Adam. The sweet Adam that was hers and the mad version of Adam when out with his mates.

Then there was the money thing. Adam was constantly skint; even after he had been paid his Jobseeker's Allowance, he would have borrowed so much and as soon as he got it, it was gone. Any extra money he earned either went down his neck or into the bookies' till. Kate was forever giving him money. She hated that he never had cash on him. Used to always seeing her dad pay for everything, it always seemed wrong that she went to the bar or she ordered the McDonalds. So before they went anywhere she would give Adam the money so he didn't feel less like a man in the relationship. Of course she never got any change.

And then there was the money he asked to borrow – £10 here, £20 there. All lent in good faith that he would pay it back. But he never did. Kate didn't earn a fortune, but she didn't spend a lot on herself, she didn't particularly go anywhere unless it was with Adam; if she wasn't seeing him, then she would just be in the house waiting! She never knew when he might want to see her.

She wore a uniform for work, so all of the clothes she bought herself were going out clothes and because it was usually just Adam she went out with, she didn't need a lot. Her friend cut her hair, she didn't smoke and her biggest luxury was her mobile phone which she had on contract. In fact she paid for two mobiles on contract; Adam had the other one. She started learning to drive, but she didn't feel like she was any good at it so packed it in and now bussed everywhere. She had declined offers of holidays with the girls, hoping that when Adam got a job, she would be able to go with him, but it didn't look like that was going to happen any time soon.

As Kate sat on her bed all these thoughts buzzed through her head. It was just after 2pm and there was still no word from Adam. They were meeting friends at 5pm so surely he would turn up soon. Had he forgotten it was her 21st birthday? She loved Adam with all of her heart, but she had the feeling that maybe her mam was right; she was stuck in a rut. She went nowhere, she did nothing. She was the one working full-time, but it was Adam, who worked rarely, that managed to get out every weekend! She had noticed that some of her friends were going to book a holiday the next day; she had the money and the holiday entitlement from work; she could go. Her friends would be over the moon if she went. *But what would Adam say? Or more to the point what would Adam do if I went?* she thought to herself. But she worked hard and had never done the girly holiday thing before!

The thoughts went around and around in her head. Maybe it would do her good, get her out of her slump. When her mobile phone buzzed the special tone for Adam, the knot in her chest expanded.

'Happy Birthday babe – really looking forward to tonight! Ring me when you get chance!' *Mmmm*, she thought. She wouldn't be ringing him straightaway, she would let him stew. But she was jittery and after five minutes she pressed the call button and her heart did the little flip thing it did whenever she heard his voice.

Ten minutes later she was in a mad rush to get ready. Adam would be there in an hour or so to pick her up. Well, he was with one of his mates; even though he had a licence he didn't have a car so more often or not one of his friends would run him round. He hadn't mentioned a present. Surely he wouldn't be giving her her present while they were out, that would be stupid. So the niggle was back; he hadn't actually got her anything!

Dressed, Kate spent half an hour sitting with her mam and dad, sipping on a glass of prosecco while she waited for Adam. Feeling that she had let them both down with refusing to go out and celebrate with the family, she suggested they all went out for Sunday lunch the following day. They were delighted and her mam was immediately texting Liam and Niall to see if they were available to go. Of course they were, they were family lads and had been brought up to respect the family and its values. She felt so bad that something as small as a lunch had brought her mam so much happiness and obviously the fact that she hadn't said that she had wanted Adam to go was an added delight for Christine.

Adam texted to say he would be 15 minutes; running upstairs to her bedroom, Kate checked herself out in the mirror. If she said it herself, she looked good. Not one for the gym, all the walking backwards and forwards to the bus stops kept her weight under control; she also had a Wii Fit that she dusted down every now and again when the mood took her. Her hair was shoulder length with a natural auburn tint; for her night out she had it piled on top of her head. She had treated herself to a new bodycon dress and she had a pair of very high sandals on. Her mam and dad had said she looked beautiful when she had gone downstairs earlier; looking in the mirror, she could see a little bit where they were coming from. She felt nice.

It turned out to be a full half an hour before Adam texted to say he was outside. He obviously wasn't coming in to collect her or to say hello to her mam and dad; he certainly didn't help the situation. But she shouted a 'bye' to her mam and dad and left the house and headed toward the Subaru Impreza parked at the kerb belong to Adam's friend Baby.

Kate liked Baby, so named because he still looked like a young teenager; of all of Adam's friends she liked Baby best. When he jumped out of the driver's seat to open the door for her, he had a bunch of flowers in his hand. She hugged and kissed him. Realising that she wouldn't want to be taking the flowers with her, he ran up to her front door, rang the bell, put the flowers on the doorstep and walked back towards the car. Her mam smiled and waved to them all as they went to pull away. Maybe she thought they were from Adam?

Adam had stayed sitting in the front seat and squeezed her knee and shouted happy birthday to her as she made herself comfortable in the back. She smiled at him; he really was good looking. Baby shouted that he thought she looked lovely; Kate could see Adam nodding but he didn't say anything! It took five minutes to get to the pub where they meeting up with Kate's friends; it probably would have taken her dad 15 minutes, but Baby drove like he was Lewis Hamilton and for most of the journey she had sat in the back with her eyes shut.

Thanking Baby for the lift and the flowers, she got out of the car and waited for Adam to finish talking to his mate before he got out of the car himself. With a toot and a roar Baby was gone. Adam grabbed Kate's hand and they made their way inside. They were a bit earlier than they had arranged and as she waited for Adam to come back from the bar, she thought it was because he wanted to give her her present before her friends arrived. It must have been a small present, mind. He wasn't carrying anything, so whatever it was it must have been in his pocket.

But when he came with the drinks he sat down and asked her what she had been doing and what she had got for her birthday. The chatting continued, no present materialised and before she knew it her friends Sophie and Jade had arrived with their boyfriends Jon-Joe and Connor and there was another round of drinks on the table, but no present from Adam.

Sophie, Jade and Kate had known each other since primary school. They were the only friends that still persisted with the reclusive Kate; they would badger and cajole her into having the odd night out with them and she loved them. The six of them would often have nights out together; Adam and Connor lived quite close to each other and whenever there was anything to celebrate they would meet up and have a night on the town. It was Sophie and Jade who were going to book their holidays the following day. Even though they both had boyfriends, they managed a week or so abroad every year. She envied them their 'bottle'!

The drinks flowed and the lads went off to have a game of pool which gave Sophie, Jade and Kate the chance to have a catch up. She knew they were going to ask what Adam had bought her; she thought about lying and then thought better of it. What was the point? Sooner or later she would drop herself in, or worse Adam would and then she would be left looking stupid. So when the inevitable question came she just said 'nothing'. Funnily enough, by just saying it, she felt better. Her friends didn't even have the decency to look shocked; they had all known Adam Mitchell for a long time and though neither Sophie nor Jade had ever said it to Kate, they thought Adam was scum of the earth and that their friend could do so much better.

Not wanting Kate to feel embarrassed, they quickly changed the subject. They talked about going to Ibiza later in the year; they were hoping to go for 10 days. As she sat and listened, Kate thought it all sounded wonderful. Sophie had recently qualified as a hairdresser; in fact she was the one who looked after Kate's hair, and Jade worked in a call centre, which she hated but paid good wages and kept them all in stitches about some of her work colleagues.

The lads came back and they made off to a livelier pub towards the centre of town. Not used to drinking so much and so early in the day, Kate's head was starting to spin and she knew that she would have to switch to soft drinks or she would be home before the night had even started. Adam was quite drunk too, no doubt he was just topping himself up from the night before. But that was him; he liked to be the life and soul of the party and the thought went through Kate's head, *What does he actually see in me?* They were just so different. But opposites attract; her own mam and dad, Christine and Mark, were very different. Christine was very outspoken and confident, she had loads of friends and liked nothing better than meeting up with them all; whereas her dad, Mark, was much quieter and preferred spending any spare time he had doing the garden or reading. They had been together for almost thirty years, so it could work.

The next pub was already packed. Kate and Jade went off to the loos while the rest went to grab a table and order drinks. Kate always had the feeling that Jade wanted to say something. She had been seeing Connor for about six months; he lived a couple of doors away from Adam and so she was sure that Jade knew something and never had the guts to tell her. She didn't want to know. The same way she stayed off Adam's Facebook page and she resisted the urge to check his mobile phone; she just didn't want to know. Even in the loos she felt under pressure. There was no way she wanted to give Jade the opportunity to tell her something, that if the truth be known she probably already knew. Adam was good looking and popular and was always out and about. Did he cheat? Probably. After all, how had they started off? He had had a long-term girlfriend when he chased after Kate and started meeting her. She didn't like to think about it and certainly didn't want to know!

The loos were busy and when a cubicle became available Kate darted into it, shutting the door behind her before Jade had chance to get in with her. She would just assume it was her time of the month and she wanted a bit of privacy, Kate thought to herself as she plonked herself down on the seat. Checking her mobile, she was surprised that there was a message from Adam. Why would he be texting her? She had only left him five minutes earlier!

Opening the text; she knew why!! 'Babe – can you do me a huge favour and lend me some money – £50 should do it – just so we can enjoy the rest of the night – I'll pay you back next week when I get my money – u look fantastic by the way – love u!' Kate sat on the loo and re-read the text. She didn't even know why she was shocked; he was always asking to borrow money; he knew she was a soft touch; that she wanted to keep him happy, and he also knew that she never expected to be paid back. She was putty in his hands. And even though she didn't want to, she knew that she didn't want him to be embarrassed in front of their friends so she would slyly pass him the money as soon as she went back into the bar.

But for the first time she was sick of it. Their relationship was very one sided, she gave – he took and she got nothing in return; she suspected that she didn't even have his loyalty. She was beginning to think more and more that her mam was right, that he was a user and a taker; that all the smooth talk was only to get what he wanted and once he had it he was away and Kate was forgotten. Tonight wasn't the night for doubts though; he was here with her and so what if it was going to cost her £50? It was for her night out too. So before she left the cubicle, she took the money out of her purse and placed it in the side pocket of her bag. She had plenty money on her; she had taken £100 out of the pile of birthday money; money she hadn't really had so wouldn't really miss.

Jade was waiting at the mirrors for her and after re-touching their make-up, they made their way back into the pub and searched around for the rest of their friends. When a pair of arms snaked around her, she knew it was Adam. He pulled her into a corner and kissed her passionately; smiling up at him, he whispered in her ear, 'Did you get my text?' She said she had and on the pretext of showing him something on her mobile, she handed him the money. The £10 note HE75 229564 that she had received earlier in the day from her Nana Rita now had a new owner.

Finding the table where the rest of her friends were sitting, Adam shortly followed her over with the drinks for them all. After about five minutes he leant over and whispered into her ear that he had to pop somewhere and wouldn't be long and then he was gone! Surely he wasn't going to get her a present now? All the shops would be shut. And he couldn't really use her money to buy her something that was just so low. She felt ill at the thought.

Connor asked where he had gone and she could answer him honestly that she didn't know. They all tried to keep the knowing looks guarded from her, but she had seen them. Was she such a fool? Another round of drinks and there was still no sign of Adam. When Jon-Joe got up to go back to the bar for another round, she knew she had to do something. Adam had been missing 45 minutes. She wasn't going to lower herself to text or ring him. She was going to just go. She had had enough, it was her 21st and here she was sitting in a pub with an absent boyfriend, who not only hadn't bought her a birthday card, or at least a present, but had borrowed money from her.

Taking out her mobile, she quickly texted her mam. The reply came back almost instantly, she would be 15 minutes. So accepting another drink, she sat for another 10 minutes or so. Adam wasn't coming back; the faces around the table were starting to look on her with pity. That would be the last time they looked at her like that. Leaning over to Sophie, she asked her what time they were going to book their holiday the next day. Happy that she could go along with them to do the booking and have lunch with the family, she stood up to leave.

No explanations were needed. She kissed each of them. Sophie said she would ring her in the morning and pick her up so that the three of them could go together to book Ibiza. And then she left the pub. Waiting outside she scoured the street for signs of Adam, there were none. But she did recognise the car that came around the corner. Jumping into the passenger seat she thought that she would cry, but the tears didn't come. Her mam didn't say anything. 'Let's just go home, Mam. The penny has finally dropped!'

3

A Bad Penny

At 24 Adam Mitchell had never done a proper day's work in his life. He didn't even look for a job, he couldn't imagine anything worse than doing the same thing day in and day out; college had been bad enough. When he went to sign on for his Jobseeker's Allowance he would go armed with a list of jobs he had applied for; well, claimed he had applied for. In truth one of Adam's friends would have listed the vacancies for the cost of a pint. Sometimes he came unstuck; there were courses he had to go on. There were ones on how to write the perfect CV, another for call centre training, but his favourite had been the forklift truck one. That had lasted for six weeks and he was now the proud owner of a certificate to say he could legally drive one. But usually the courses were just to be endured or else his payment would be stopped.

He earned money though, he would pick up the odd day's work here and there, he didn't mind; there was always cash at the end of the day and if he had cash he had fun. Adam hadn't intended to live his life like this. At school he had been really smart. He had been captain of his year's football team and excelled at maths and science. That was until he was about 14 and had been introduced to drink and drugs and women, then school held no appeal for him and he went less and less. By the time he officially left he didn't have a single qualification to his name.

Looking back even he knew he had been stupid. Today when he had been out with Connor Bell he knew that the path that he had chosen in comparison to Connor's had been the wrong one. Connor had gone on to sixth form and then university and now was an engineer. He had a brand new car, wore nice clothes and by the looks of it an abundance of credit cards in his wallet. Oh, and he had just put a deposit down on a house. Adam had nothing.

Jack the lad about town wasn't really enough. He made out he was happy with his lot, but was far from it. Everything was a show. He had nothing and if he carried on the way he was going he would never have nothing; if he lived that long, that was. The binge drinking was getting out of control and then there was the occasional drugs he used. He didn't think he had a problem with the drugs, but he would if he didn't stop using soon. The drink was definitely a problem. He drank too much because he was miserable and he was miserable because he drank. The money he wasted on a night out was ridiculous. He was ridiculous. He robbed Peter to pay Paul, then did it all over again. His mam was sick of him and after today's performance he knew that he had blown it with Kate.

He felt sick. Poor Kate, it was her 21st birthday.

His mam, bless her, had given him some money to go and buy her a present yesterday afternoon, but true to form he didn't even get to the shops to buy her anything. There seemed to be better things to spend the money on. But that was yesterday and today he was having to live with the consequences. He didn't deserve her. She was lovely, too lovely, and because she was lovely he took advantage of her. She had been the best thing in his life for the past few years and he betrayed her time after time. Kate always saw the best in him, she only wanted to make him happy. But he took advantage of her and even when he vowed to himself he wouldn't do it again, there was always something he wanted to do with his friends and Kate was the one way he could do it.

Look what he had just done! He had taken money off Kate on the pretence that it was for the rest of the night out and that's what he had intended to do when he had texted her earlier. But then when he was at the bar one of his mates had texted; he had a 'dead cert' for a greyhound running that night and he asked Adam to meet him at the bookies. At first he had said no. But then Connor had come to the bar and insisted that he pay for the drinks that Adam had ordered. Furious and humiliated, even though he knew Connor wasn't trying to make him feel crap, he had sat at the table with the other five and suddenly the £50 in his pocket was starting to burn. If the dog was a sure thing then the £50 would be about £700 and then he would give Kate her money back and go out and buy her a present the next day.

She looked so beautiful sitting there. She was smiling at him, even after she had given him money she still loved him. The others at the table didn't look at him so lovingly though, especially Jade, Connor's girlfriend. She saw straight through him; no doubt Connor had filled her in on his antics, and Connor must have seen Jessie Carr leaving his house that lunchtime. He hadn't meant it to happen; he never did. But he couldn't help himself, a belly full of beer and a couple of uppers and he was away. He had known Jessie for years but last night was the first time he had taken her home. She wasn't even that nice, not a patch on Kate and she had a terrible reputation, but that hadn't seemed to matter last night; or should he say this morning because he was sure it was getting light when the two of them had fallen out of a taxi and into his house.

Jessie in daylight resembled nothing of Jessie of the night. There was fake tan all over his sheets, his skin had been glistening with the stuff and with her hair extensions out and her fake eyelashes off, she wasn't a pretty sight, he thought to himself as he did the gentlemanly thing and made her tea and toast in bed. His mam had been furious with him; she really liked Kate and told Adam in no uncertain terms what a bastard he was and that she wanted 'that trollop' out of the house.

Watching Jessie walk down the path to the waiting taxi, he saw Connor's car pull up and park. He would have been blind not to have seen her or more alarmingly where she had been. The look that Jade was giving him as he sat with Kate said it all. He thought about pulling her to one side and telling her to keep quiet, but she didn't seem to have said anything to Kate anyway, and they had just been to the loos together and that would have been an opportunity for Jade to put the boot in. He felt like he had kicked a puppy; even though Kate was oblivious he still felt like shit.

The thing was though, it hadn't been the first time. Most weekends would find him in some girl's bed, the mistake he had made was taking Jessie home with him. He didn't know why he did it, he was a flirt sober but he would never dream of cheating on Kate, but a few drinks, the beat of the music and barely dressed girls would find him in the mood. Instead of going home or going to Kate, he would end up wrapped around some girl he had no intention of ever seeing again. A lot of it was bravado; loser Adam with no job or money needed to be a success at something; and pulling seemed to be it.

He knew he was good looking, he was told often enough and he never had any trouble chatting up girls. But even Adam was smart enough to know that his looks would fade, especially with his drink and drug consumption, then what would he be and what would he have? So while he still had it, he used it. Kate wouldn't leave him, he was sure of that; or would she? His mam had really done a job on him earlier that day. The door had hardly closed on Jessie and his mam just went ballistic. Firstly for spending Kate's birthday money and then for cheating on her. She left him in no uncertain terms what he was and what would happen to him. Kate would leave, she said. And she had gone on about how she hadn't brought him up to be the bum he had turned into. How many times the police had been to the door. It had gone on and on.

He hated upsetting his mam and to see her so distraught destroyed him. His dad had walked out on them when he was just a toddler and his sister Kay-Lee was five, and his mam had done a good job; at least with Kay-Lee anyway. She wasn't living at home anymore, had moved out a few months earlier to live with her boyfriend. But she was hard working and honest, just like his mam. Adam had obviously taken after his dad. He had chased every bit of skirt he could find until one day he had chased the wrong one and got himself chased out of town, but not until after he had taken a beating from his latest floozy's husband. He had gone and never came back. There had been no Christmas or birthday cards but that didn't mean they missed out. His granddad and mam had made sure that didn't happen. His granddad had been the dad he never had and when he died when Adam was 14, that was the start of his decline.

No, that wasn't true, that wasn't the reason; it was a coincidence really, but he did sometimes wonder if his granddad hadn't died when he did he might not have got into as much trouble. His Granddad was a force to be reckoned with. But he did die and Adam met a group of older lads who were much more interesting than the lads he had knocked about with up until then. Suddenly his classmates were tame. They didn't drink or play truant and they certainly hadn't discovered the other sex. All of a sudden there was a new world open to Adam and he dived into it head-first. His mam didn't know what had hit her. One day she had a loving young boy, the next she had an out-of-control teenager.

The police were always picking him up and

bringing him home; he wasn't trouble to them, but he should have been in school instead of roaming the roads swigging on a cheap bottle of cider. He liked to be the centre of attention and so became the joker in the pack; and of course he was a hit with the girls. Blond hair and blue eyes, the ladies adored him and he adored them. He liked sex, what he didn't like was being tied down to just one and within months had a reputation for being a bit of a ladies' man, or in his case a ladies' boy. It didn't stop his fun, there were plenty of girls only too willing to give themselves to him; almost all of them in the hope that they would be the one.

Sooner or later though the inevitable happened and he started to get himself into some petty crime. Usually cars; he was banned from driving even before he had his provisional licence. Each time he was taken to court, he escaped a custodial sentence by the skin of his teeth. He took whatever punishment they gave him and moved on, promising his probation officer that he wouldn't get into trouble again. But of course it didn't last; right up until just before his 18th birthday when he was arrested for stealing yet another car. This time it was serious and whereas before it would have been a juvenile facility, this time he would be sentenced as an adult.

Adam was terrified. Suddenly it was all very serious and the chances of him getting away with it this time were slim. He was terrified and his worst fears became a reality when he was sentenced to two years in prison, suspended for six months. He had a reprieve. And he really did try to turn his life around. He got himself a steady girlfriend and went to college, but at the end of the course there was no job for him, even with a qualification in plumbing. And before he knew it he was back to his old ways, maybe even worse.

He constantly cheated on Trudy; she had her own place and he used it like a hotel. Between Trudy's and his mam's he wanted for nothing. He would get £20 from his mam and then go around and tell Trudy his mam had asked for £20 that he had borrowed the week before. With £40 in his pocket he would hit the town; drunk and high by the following morning, he would be in someone else's house, in someone else's bed.

Then he met Kate at a mate's 21st birthday party. A bit drunk when he got there, she was the birthday boy's little sister and from the minute he saw her he couldn't take his eyes off her. She was sweet and pretty and shy; a million miles away from the girls he was used to. But she agreed to dance with him and once he was with her he didn't want to let her go, he didn't even bother having another drink; she was all the intoxication he needed and he knew he wanted to see her again.

So he sent her a message and lo and behold she replied. Not that he hadn't expected her to, but it had been a day or so since the party and he was sure that Niall would have warned her off him. They arranged to meet and for the first time in his life, he wasn't in a rush. She reminded him of his mam; not looks wise, but in her nature, even only knowing him a few days he could see the devotion in her eyes. She was special and he hated having to sneak around with her in case Trudy found out; Kate wasn't the least bit confrontational and even Adam felt ill at the thought of Trudy having a go at her.

Eventually it sorted itself out, or he was caught out. A night in town, another willing girl and the next day it was plastered all over Facebook. A furious Trudy had had enough and dumped him very publicly. He and Trudy had been good while they lasted, but it had ran its course and thanks to a girl whose name he couldn't remember, he could be with his Kate.

She really was the nicest person he had ever met. And he did try; but he didn't have a job and she did so he would spend his days kicking his heels when she was at work and the only people who were around through the day were lads in the same position as him. And with little money it was very easy to revert to type and start doing little jobs again. Of course Kate knew nothing about that side of Adam. She knew he was unreliable, but she had assumed that he went out on the drink all the time; he didn't. Usually he would just go out one or two nights a week. The other nights he would be doing something dodgy for a few extra quid.

Kate was good and trusting and kind and he didn't deserve her. The more he thought he didn't deserve her the more bad things he did. He didn't mean to; he didn't want to hurt her, but the drink and the drugs would kick in and he would be off again. She would be the last thing on his mind as he chased after some 'Jordan' wannabe. He knew himself that he was pathetic and that day's performance proved it.

What sort of person would take money off his girlfriend and then do one? His mam was right, he was the lowest of the low and she had said that even before he had done what he had just done. With any luck he could be back in the pub with Kate in half an hour; hopefully with a pocket full of money.

Trots, his mate with the tip, was in the bookies when Adam arrived. The dog he had had a tip for was running in the 7.06 race, a sure thing, Trots said; he knew the kennel maid and she had told him that the little bitch was good to go that night and to get some money on it. It was straight from the horse's mouth, so to speak. Trots had stuck a tenner on it. Adam checked the odds showing on the television screen – 25/1; £250.00 if he put on a tenner. Not a bad half hour's work and he would be able to give Kate her £50 back and buy her a present and pay for the rest of their night out. He smiled. He had ballsed up with Jessie, but Kate didn't know and it looked like Jade wasn't going to say anything so he had chance to make things up to her without her even knowing. He felt quite happy as he stood in the queue waiting to put on the bet. He had a second chance; or more like a second hundredth chance and this time he wasn't going to blow it. He would text Kate as soon as the race finished and tell her he was on his way back.

But standing at the counter he had a change of heart. £250.00 was okay, but if he put the £50 on he would have over a grand, that would properly sort him out. The dog was a sure thing, even its name, Hope to Do, was encouraging. By the time it was his turn his mind was made up. Fifty quid win on number six dog – Hope to Do, handing over the crispy notes which included HE75 229564, which Kate had been given that morning and had subsequently handed over to Adam. The deed was done. Debs, who was one of the regular cashiers there, looked at him in horror. Obviously it wasn't her place to say anything, but she knew Adam and she knew he didn't have money to throw around. He saw her look and smiled. Hope to Do was a dead cert; he had no worries.

And he could hardly contain his excitement as he watched the dogs being loaded into the traps. Dog six was tiny; she looked like a puppy in comparison to the other dogs, but Trots said she went like a rocket; or she would tonight. All of a sudden Adam had doubts. What had he done?

The hare was off; the trap doors opened and the dogs all went flying after the stuffed toy they called the hare. Trots was right; she was a little rocket; she took off and was a good six feet in front of the next dog. 'Come on, my beauty!' Adam shouted at the screen. She looked like she was running for her life. And then it was over. Too fast for the bend, she took a tumble and the other five dogs went past her. Hope to Do had been hopeless; she had lost her race and he had lost his money, or more specifically Kate's money.

He was speechless, or seething, whatever it was he was feeling he couldn't move. He watched the screen as Hope to Do's kennel maid put her back on her lead and walked her off the track back to the kennels. Trots had disappeared the minute the dog fell; just as well really because Adam wanted to punch him. Dead cert? The anger was bubbling up inside him and he knew that sometime soon the red mist would settle in front of his eyes and he would be lost in a huge ball of aggression.

He could see Debs looking at him. She must have

thought he was going to kick off; he was, but it wouldn't be in the bookies. He smiled a thin smile and left. Not sure what to do with himself he sat on the wall outside and waited for his anger to calm. Checking his mobile phone, there were no messages from Kate. He had been gone almost an hour; she was either having a really good time and hadn't thought about how long he had been gone or she had given up on him. He thought the latter. When the mobile started ringing he thought it might be Kate, but no, it was Joe Swan. More bad news.

Joe Swan had been a friend of his for years, he would often put the odd 'job' Adam's way. But he was bad news and a phone call from him meant he had some dodgy deal he wanted Adam to do for him. The thing was that he always paid well, so that showed the calibre of the job. He thought about not answering. He wouldn't normally on a Saturday night, but now he had no money and wouldn't dare face Kate as it was. He clicked answer.

Half an hour later he was in a pub sitting with Joe, Trots and a couple of Joe's lackeys who he knew vaguely. Trots must have told him about Adam losing the money in the bookies and Joe had thought he would cash in on it; he was like that, Joe, preyed on the desperate. The short of it was he needed someone to drive one of the lackeys into the city centre with a parcel. Adam wasn't stupid, he knew what Joe was about and if he needed someone else to drive then it must be something dodgy that needed delivering. And if he needed any more proof that it was more than likely drugs he was moving, the offer of £100 to do the job clarified it. He couldn't refuse. £100 would pay Kate her money back and get her a little present. If he was lucky there might be £20 left for him, but at least he could save face a bit and at the end of the day he had little choice.

So he and Luke the lackey set off in the Vauxhall Vectra; it didn't bother Adam that he was carrying drugs, he had moved worse in his time; or that the car that he was driving probably had no insurance, let alone was insured for him to drive. The whole job would take an hour, tops. All he had to do was drive into the city centre and wait while Luke the lackey went into a club and then bring him back, park up the car and get his money. A different night to what he had planned but then most nights were for him.

But the red mist still hadn't cleared; it wasn't as red now, but there was still a pink hue. He was annoyed at himself, at the bloody dog and even at Kate. If she wasn't so kind and generous none of this would have happened; he wouldn't have put 50 quid on a dog and lost and he wouldn't be driving into town with a parcel of drugs for the scumbag Joe.

Thinking he might just be able to get back to the pub before Kate left and somehow try and make it up to her, he put his foot down. In the pink haze he didn't see the red light he jumped or the blue light from the car behind. It wasn't until he heard the siren that he realised there was even a police car behind him. He thought to put his foot down and flee, but it was a shitty Vectra he was driving and he would get nowhere. He slowed down and went to pull in. Luke the lackey, sensing what was going to happen opened the passenger door and ran. Adam did nothing. He was sitting in what was probably a stolen car, with no insurance and a parcel of drugs. Before the police even got to the door he knew he was done for. He wound down the window, put his head against the steering wheel and waited.

'Can you step outside the car, sir?' the voice said. He had no option, he got out of the car and leant against the bonnet. He knew the policeman; he'd been arrested by him before. 'If it isn't Adam Mitchell. You're like a bad penny. You always turn up sooner or later, son!' The mist had cleared, but he still couldn't see. Not because of the red or the pink. He couldn't see because of the tears that stung the back of his eyes, the tears that he was desperately trying not to let go. He was a lad about town, not a cry baby. But what did it matter anymore? In his head he started to scream, *Kate*…

4

Hand to Mouth

Debs Johnston couldn't get Adam Mitchell out of her mind. Not because he was young or good looking or flirty; he was all of those things. No, it was because she had taken his bet and then had watched him lose. She had seen the look on his face both when he put the bet on and then again when the dog had taken a tumble. She had willed the dog to win, but like all the things you wished for, you seldom got. She liked Adam; she had known him for years. Some said he was trouble, but she had always found him pleasant enough, he'd just got in with the wrong crowd and once you were in with them it was hard to get out.

She did think he was going to kick off in the shop, he might have done if Trots had stayed, but the little weasel had gone the minute the dog fell; from what she had heard the dog had been his tip, so it was just as well he had made a sharp exit if the look on Adam's face was anything to go by. Adam never bet big. She had known him come in and put the odd fiver on a football coupon, but when he handed her

50 quid, she had been shocked. A couple of conversations later and she knew why; Trots was chasing a bit of skirt that worked at the kennels. He was a creepy boy and no doubt the lass had given him duff information just to get him off her back. It was a good job it hadn't won really because she would never have got shot of him.

But she couldn't shake Adam out of her head. It was part of the job, taking money off punters and more often than not, giving them nothing back in return. It wasn't her job to tell people not to. But she had really wanted to say something to Adam; she knew he didn't work and really couldn't afford such a big luxury of losing it. But she hadn't, she had given him one of her withering looks and he had taken no notice. Best she just forget about it.

It was the likes of Adam Mitchell that paid her wages. She saw them come in day in and day out. Sometimes they would get lucky, but usually they would leave with empty pockets. The only winner in bookies was the bookies. It was a mug's game. She had worked there for almost 10 years and not only had the premises changed dramatically, so had the clientele.

At 37 Debs looked 47 and most days felt 100. She had three kids at home and no husband or even a partner. She hadn't set off to be a single mam, it had just happened more by bad luck than bad management, or should she say bad judgement. Each of her three children – Declan 14, Rory 12 and Jasper 9 – had different dads. Three relationships resulting in three children; three men and three boys. Was three her lucky number? She adored her boys but they were hard work. She thought that the hard work would be over as soon as each of them started school, but that was just the beginning. Now the pressure she was under just to clothe and feed them was unbelievable and like all kids, they wanted what their mates had.

That was why three days and two nights a week she worked in the bookies. It wasn't ideal with kids, but the wages were quite good and it was on her doorstep so there were no travel expenses to pay. She liked her job, she liked the people she worked with and she even liked some of the punters; they would often tip her a fiver here and there if they had a win. And every penny helped.

When she first started working there it had been a family-run concern. It was called Brough's the Bookmakers and it was third generation. It was old-fashioned and bets were worked out manually; that was one of the reasons she had got the job, she could add up quickly which was an asset in that line of work. The Broughs were a lovely family to work for; they cared about their staff and there were always presents for the kids at Christmas and a little something for their birthdays and Easter. But like everything, the big boys came and made them an offer they couldn't refuse; she didn't blame them, it was getting to be a harder and harder trade for them what with all the electronic games and the internet; something the Broughs would never think of installing. The most technical thing they had in the shop was a bandit and they weren't even keen on that and had only got it because the punters wanted something to do in-between races.

So the Broughs sold up and the shop closed for two weeks only to re-open a replica of every other bookmakers in the country and with a whole load of technology that Debs and her workmates had had to be sent away to train on. It was a completely different place to work; the old punters complained constantly, even with the complimentary teas and coffees they weren't happy. They missed the intimacy of the old shop and so did Debs. Now she wasn't a person, she was a faceless identification number on a payroll; they knew nothing about her and even the manager that came to oversee the shop spent more time staring at his computer than he did with his staff and he certainly didn't interact with the customers.

And even the customers changed. The new roulette-type machines that buzzed and pinged all day attracted the youngsters in who on payday would think nothing of blowing £100 in five minutes on the brightly lit machines. At first mortified, Debs soon lost interest in the idiots who thought that the next tenner would bring them riches. She would watch them go backwards and forwards to the cash machine that had been installed in the corner, which really took the mick because on top of the fact that they were probably going to lose the withdrawn money in the roulette machine, the cashpoint had the audacity to charge them £1.94 for the privilege.

It wasn't just youngsters though; women started coming into the shop. They would come in and take a complimentary cup of coffee and then go and park their backside at one of the machines for half an hour. Not used to seeing women coming in and out of the shop, she was fascinated. It was something that she would certainly have never done and for the years before the only women that had come in had been either putting a bet on for someone else or one of the four or five regular women who liked a flutter on the Grand National or Gold Cup; the women that used the machines were alien to her.

But she got to know them. Many were single mams like herself, trying to make a few extra quid where they could. They would come in, spend a tenner; if they won, fantastic, if they lost they would have to pull back somewhere else in the family budget. It was a chance to make some extra money and she got that. She would do the same herself, but the risk that the ten would turn into twenty and so on put the fear of God into her. She had seen it happen so often. Not with the women, mind, they were usually sensible. But she had seen men do it.

They would bet and lose and then try and double up on the next bet and so it went on. She had seen grown men cry because they had emptied their bank account of mortgage and rent money; some just didn't know when to stop and would risk everything on the off chance that today was their day. It seldom happened and Deb's heart would break. It didn't matter who they were or how stupid they had been, everything in the shop pointed to winnings and wealth; it was a business and she could see how easy it was for people to get sucked into the whole 'win big' mentality.

It gave her sleepless nights. Just like Adam Mitchell would have that night. She didn't mean to take her job home with her, but sometimes when she knew that something life-changing had happened, it would hang on her for days. Even if they won. She had once had someone win over £30,000 on an accumulator; she had taken the bet and she had still been in the shop when the fifth horse had romped home. A good day for the punter; a terrible day for the bookie, but it happened. Not always that much but enough to cause the bookmaker some heartache and give Debs a smile. She loved it when the underdog won. But days like that were few and far between and mostly the punters lost and the bookmaker won. You only had to look around the fixtures and fittings in the shop to know who the winners were.

The job kept the wolf from the door though and to some extent kept Debs sane. Her boys would make a saint swear and sometimes it did her good to get away from them. Her mam and dad helped out a lot with childcare, but on a Saturday they liked to go to the local club so she had to have a sitter in. Her neighbour's daughter Amy was the latest in a long line of babysitters, not because they were naughty for them, just because the sitters would grow up and want to go out themselves on a Saturday night. Because it was the only day of the week that she needed someone to keep an eye on them, she could afford to pay good rates, so the turnover of babysitters was probably slower than she would have expected. Amy had been with her since she was 15 and she was now 18 so not only were the boys used to her, Debs knew that Amy could be trusted.

Out of the three men she had had children with, there was only Jasper's dad, Carl, still about. He was a good bloke and would take all the boys if she got stuck for childcare. With a young family of his own with his new partner, she was grateful for the help he gave, especially with the older two. Both their dads were long gone; Rory's before the baby had even put in an appearance. Declan's dad, Derek, just didn't take to fatherhood, or at least that was what he had said when she arrived from the shops one day to find her hallway packed with black plastic bags full of his things. She didn't even get chance to talk to him about it before he was out of the door, packing his car and away. That was the last she saw of him. They had been together five years; she thought he was 'it' but he turned out to be more of a 'tit'! He had broken her heart and on the rebound she had met John.

The whole thing with John had been quick and intense and she was pregnant within months. As soon as the two blue lines showed up on the pregnancy test, John was up and away. Everything suddenly got a lot worse; she was pregnant again and with a toddler already in tow, she felt very, very alone. She thought about a termination; she thought long and hard. She thought so long and hard, it got past the point of no return. So with only the support of her mam and dad, Debs gave birth to Rory. Holding him in her arms, she was pleased she had him.

But it was hard. With both dads absent she relied totally on her benefits to survive. Her mam and dad would help where they could, but they didn't have much and often it was a case of her mam turning up with a pan of broth or a pie – it was the best she could do. Every little helped though and Debs always tried to make up in love and attention for what they missed out on in material things. She got herself a little bar job, but she had to be careful how many hours she worked or else they would be cutting her benefits. Her mam and dad were her saving grace, they would look after the kids on the nights she worked so even the pittance that she earned in the pub made a difference. When word got around that Brough's the Bookmakers were looking for a cashier, Debs knew it was the job for her.

So the following day she trundled off to the Jobcentre and spoke to her adviser at length. The job being advertised was full-time; yes, her benefits would be stopped, but there would be other things she would be entitled to as a full-time working single mam. It gave her hope. She would apply for the job and if she was lucky enough to get it, then she would go back with all the hours and wages and talk to her adviser again.

Debs had never been in a bookies before, but it wasn't as if she was going to put a bet on; so with her head held high, she pushed open the door and made her way through the dense cigarette smoke to the counter. The gentleman who greeted her when her turn came could be no other than Mr Brough; all of a sudden she was very nervous. She explained the reason for her visit and smiling kindly at her, he ushered her into the back room, where his wife was sitting working on a ledger. As she took down some details, Debs warmed to her straightaway. Explaining that there was a very basic application form to fill in, she then said that there would be a small test to ascertain Debs' maths skills.

The application form proved tricky to fill in, but she flew through the maths test. Mrs Brough beamed at her; she had been the best applicant they had seen and if she was willing, then the job was hers. It had been that easy. Armed with all the facts and figures she needed, she made her way back to the Jobcentre to see her adviser, who seemed to be as delighted as she was and after a couple of telephone calls, she confirmed that by working full-time, Debs would be about £100 a week better off. Not a lot for working 37 hours a week. But it was £100 and if she could get help from her mam and dad with regards to childcare, it would be like having a small fortune every week.

And that was the start of her employ at Brough's. Her mam and dad were fantastic and refused to take any money off her when she offered it to them for taking care of Declan and Rory. Instead she would buy them bits of food when she did her own shopping. The only thing they asked was that when she worked on a Saturday, they only have the boys until teatime so that they could still go out for a few drinks on a Saturday night. That was fine with Debs; she couldn't exactly complain and she sought a babysitter for the few hours the boys needed watching.

It all worked out well. She loved her job from the minute she took her first bet. Even though it wasn't her money, the adrenalin was contagious and she would will her regular customers to win big. Some were generous and she would often be given a little something for the boys; every penny extra made a huge difference to her. She really liked working for the Brough's; they appreciated her and she learnt so much from them. She liked them so much that by the time her benefits were sorted she didn't have as much extra as her Jobcentre adviser had predicted – less than half – but she loved her job and didn't want to let the Broughs down by leaving. £50 a week plus the odd tips was better than nothing.

Carl was a regular; if she thought about it Adam

Mitchell reminded Debs of him. He was a bit of a Jack the lad, always up to something, but Debs liked him and would look out for him coming into the bookies when she was on shift. He flirted outrageously with her and in turn she would bat her eyelids back at him. But he was younger than her. She already had two young boys in her life, she didn't need another one. The flirting continued though and when he cheekily asked her one night to go out for a drink with him, she meant to take the wind out of his sails by saying yes, but secretly she really wanted to go. It had been so long since she had had any male attention and Carl Steers was certainly a bit of eye candy for the ladies.

He didn't seem shocked that she had said yes, just chuffed to bits. In the end they had gone for a curry and had a really good night. He wasn't half as cocky when he was on his own, he was quite shy and really interesting. There were eight years between them and even though they got on really well, it was only ever going to be a bit of fun; a night out here and there when Debs could get a sitter, but of course it turned physical and when she felt a wave of nausea come over he one day, she knew she had been caught out again. This time there was no way she could keep it; she had no money as it was, never mind having to have time off for maternity leave and then have an extra mouth to feed.

She told Carl; she couldn't not, that wasn't her way. He agreed, there was no way he was ready to be a dad. He got on well with Declan and Rory but only saw them for short spells from time to time. Even her GP had no hesitation in referring her and within a week everything was in place. But the night before she couldn't sleep. She had been brought up with morals and values and one of the things that had been instilled in her was that abortion was a sin. She spent the night tossing and turning, getting out of bed and drinking tea and eating biscuits. She watched Declan and Rory sleeping and was eaten up with guilt; it wasn't the baby's fault. By morning she knew that she couldn't go through with it and as she was leaving the house to take the boys to school, Carl was coming through the gate. She knew as soon as she saw him that he felt the same.

By the time Jasper put in an appearance, she was ready for him. She had worked right up to her due date so she could have a bit longer maternity leave if she needed it and she and Carl had a strange sort of togetherness about them; they weren't a couple, but he was there for her. And he had been generous to a fault, helping buy baby equipment and giving Debs little bits of cash when he could afford it. They weren't a couple by any means, in fact he had a new girlfriend who he seemed really keen on. The fact that Debs was having his baby didn't seem to faze Emma and she would often pop over to Debs' if Carl was coming over. She still liked Carl a lot, but it was never going to be more than it was and she liked Emma, which she was pleased about because the baby would be spending a lot of time with her in the future.

Her mam and dad weren't so happy with the situation; three kids to three different men was disgusting. But they were her mam and dad and apart from a brother she had living in Aberdeen who turned up a couple of times a year, Debs and the boys were all they had. And Jasper brought so much love with him; with his bright blond hair he looked like an angel, even if he didn't sound like one. Somehow she managed. She went back to work earlier than she should have; money was tight and she really didn't have a lot of choice. The SMP she got was a pittance and even with the little extra Carl paid her every week, it was still a struggle.

But Carl was a good dad. He would take the boys out together so Declan and Rory didn't feel left out; even if it was just to McDonalds, he wouldn't leave the older boys out if he could help it. When Emma got pregnant herself, they were all excited. They were a menagerie of a family, but it worked. Grandma, Granddad, the boys, Debs, Carl, Emma and eventually their three little girls. If Jasper didn't call them Mam and Dad, you would have thought Debs and Carl were brother and sister; close but not close. Most Christmases would find them all together; different but nice.

Debs continued to work hard. But the boys were growing so fast. She just seemed to buy them a pair of trainers and they would outgrow them or they would wreck them. Christmas and birthdays were a nightmare; if she didn't use a doorstep weekly loan company she would have no chance of even getting them anything. There was never a spare penny to save.

Twice a year she would borrow £1,500. This was always kept for birthdays and Christmas and she would try her best not to use it for anything else. Every week Joyce the doorstep collector would come and collect her weekly payment. It was Debs' only chance of survival in the 'treat' department;

something that seemed to be getting more and more expensive every year as the boys grew and they asked for more and more extravagant presents like their mates were getting. It worried her. She managed at the minute, but she knew she was going to have to start borrowing more in the future, putting an even tighter grip on her finances. But they were her boys and she wanted them to be happy and certainly not left behind their other friends.

She had a catalogue now. She only used it to buy the boys clothes; she had always managed to just buy cheap in the past; they were never bothered what they wore, but now they were asking for named stuff. For the price of one thing she could have had each of them virtually kitted out. She couldn't afford it, so had taken on a catalogue so that at least she could get them the odd named thing; a pair of trainers or a hoodie. She paid over the odds for everything, but she had no choice and paying it back weekly was the only way she could afford to do it.

And then there was the cash they asked for; even a trip to the pictures cost £20 each. She always tried to let them go places with school friends, but sometimes she had to say no and then there would be hell on. More often than not she gave in and would have to cut back somewhere else and then spend the rest of the week trying to catch up with herself. That was why she was always so grateful when one of the punters gave her a little something out of their winnings; it took the pressure off again.

She had a new man in her life. She had met him online but he lived 200 miles away. He had been up a few times, but as yet she hadn't had chance to go down and see him; every time she had just about got the money together for her coach fare, something else would happen and she would have to dip into it to pay. Paul was nice though and didn't put any pressure on her. He said he didn't mind driving up once a month to see her, but how long would that last? It was more of a virtual relationship than a physical one. Phone calls and texts; he said he understood, but she knew deep down someone else would come along and he would be gone.

They had been talking to each other for about eight months, met three times and that was the total sum of their relationship. She didn't think he was a player, but what did she know about men? Carl had turned out to be a gem, but he wasn't her gem and the other two were distant memories. Paul offered to pay but she was too proud; even though he had a good job and owned his own home and car, she couldn't let him pay to see her. It didn't feel right. So for the minute she made do with the phone calls and the texts and the odd visit up to her house, knowing that sooner or later he would get fed up and move on. There was nothing she could do!

Her shift was coming to an end. It had been a long and busy day; there had been a couple of big race meetings and lots of football, the shop had been fit to burst most of the day. The amount of money that had gone through her hands was obscene. And then there was Adam Mitchell, who she really couldn't shake off. He was an idiot but she knew he had been sucked in to do something he usually wouldn't do and she was worried about what he would do; he looked so mad…

Just as she was starting to cash up, one of her

regulars came in. He was in every day, sometimes twice or thrice; he was one of those ones who was always chasing his tail. Debs knew he had a wife and young family, but would watch him go backwards and forwards to the cash machine getting more money so he could try and win his losses back. As irresponsible as he was, she liked Jake. His heart was in the right place but just like hundreds like him, he hadn't woken up and realised what a mug's game gambling was. This time he had a winning slip, a football bet where his predicted scores had all come in. Nice one, £947.22. She was pleased she hadn't actually done her 'end of day' or she would have had to start it all over again. She smiled as she handed over his winnings and he beamed back at her. She was pleased for him. In with his winning was a £10 note, HE75 229564, and as he went to put the money in his wallet, he handed over the note to her, telling her to treat her boys. Like most punters in the bookies, he knew all about Debs and her boys. She was so grateful and slipped the note into her pocket. Company policy stated that she wasn't supposed to accept gratuities from customers, but when she worked for the Brough's they had encouraged it, it was one of the things she wasn't giving up and would tell them so if they ever pulled her, perk of the job!

A very happy Jake left the shop and Debs and her colleague cashed up, shut down the machines and televisions and made the place secure. It had been a long day and she was delighted to be standing watching the shutters come down at the end of her shift. She had two days off now and was looking forward to doing the mundane stuff like her washing and ironing and the thankless task she called housework. She had to call and get some shopping on the way home, so made her way across to the open-all-hours supermarket, Singh's.

She had long ago stopped doing a weekly big shop; the boys were like a plague of locusts and the food that should have lasted them a week was gone in two days. They would eat her out of house and home if they had chance. Even though the big supermarkets were cheaper, she made do with the local convenience stores where she paid extra, but bought only enough for a day or two and at that time of night she would often be able to pick up something that was reduced; she had an ever evolving menu depending what she could buy cheaply.

Making her way around the little supermarket, she thanked God for her maths skills. She only had £20 to spend, more than she had originally had thanks to Jake, but still it wouldn't go far so she had to be careful. But they had a few things with short dates reduced and she got some bacon and some mince at half the price she would have originally paid for them. She felt happy, she would make a pan of broth and a bolognaise; the boys loved both and if she got an extra loaf, they would make a meal out of the broth for a couple of days. Her biggest extravagance was washing powder that she seemed to buy every other day; she only ever bought the small one; the big one was too expensive and too bulky to carry, so she made do with the little one, same with milk and everything else she seemed to use at a rapid pace. She had to buy small and often.

Mr Singh took her basket off her and rang everything up on his till. He had owned the shop for as long as she could remember and always had a ready smile for his customers. He knew her and he knew her boys; when Declan had tried to buy cigarettes, he had had a quiet word with Debs. Declan said they had been for a mate and because he was the biggest in the group and the oldest looking, he had got the job of going into the shop. But the silly bugger should have known Mr Singh knew who he was and how old he was, but she was grateful for the word in the ear and would keep an eye on Declan just in case he was smoking.

£18.32; she was a pound out, but then she had lost concentration when she was rummaging through the reduced section. On an impulse she asked Mr Singh for a scratch card – a £2 one – and handed him over the extra money along with two £10 notes, one of them being HE75 229564. She didn't usually buy scratch cards, but maybe some of Jake's luck would rub off on her and she would be lucky. She pushed it into one of the bags that Mr Singh passed to her; she would keep it for later, after she had made the pan of broth and the spaghetti bolognaise.

'Hope you are lucky!' Mr Singh cheerily said as she was leaving.

'Me too. You know what it's like. Hand to mouth, Mr Singh. Something has to give!' She smiled and made for the door. Off home to pay her babysitter and feed her boys and eventually put her feet up and watch a bit of telly. It had been a long hard day.

5

Look After the Pennies and the Pounds

Will Look After Themselves

M r Singh watched the woman that worked in the bookmakers leave. He didn't know her name but he knew her and her family and he knew that life was a struggle for her. He would watch her on the CCTV camera as she searched through the reduced section for things she could use. She was good, mind; she was obviously good at keeping a running total and always had just about the right amount of money out ready to pay.

She wasn't the only one who used his shop that lived – what did she call it? – 'hand to mouth'! Times were hard for many; the amount of times he credited gas and electric cards for £1.50 or £2.00; it was heart-breaking. He helped as best he could; he would often reduce the prices on items long before he should do, just so the little section he kept for the reductions always had choice. It wasn't all charity, mind; it was also a good business ploy; just like selling his essential items cheap. They came in for the cheap stuff, but then they would also pick up things that they needed at full price. It kept the customers coming through the door and any reductions were written off through his books. At the end of the day he was a businessman and he needed to make money to keep the shop going.

Ravi Singh was as English as English. Born in the Midlands, his father and his father before him had all been shopkeepers; though he was the first generation to be born in England. He had a twin brother, Sandhu, who also ran a convenience store, but his was in the south and he had two younger sisters who had both gone into medicine. The amount of aunts, uncles and cousins he had scattered about the country was staggering, but somehow they all managed to keep in touch with each other.

A family of his own now, his wife Mani, son Kal and daughter Mena all worked in the family business. It was just as well; the shop opened at 7am and closed at 11pm, it needed to be kept stocked and the till manned. It was hard work for them all. And getting harder as money got tighter and tighter. The family running the business alone kept the overheads down and they had the added convenience of living on the premises with the flat they lived in being upstairs.

He had a good family; as was the tradition he had an arranged marriage but Mani had turned out to be a dream and they were just about to celebrate 25 very happy years together. They had been lucky. He had friends whose arranged marriages hadn't worked out quite as well and were living miserable existences; divorce was very much a no-no still. But he loved Mani and she loved him. She was his business partner and his best friend; they had been blessed. His children were very English and he knew that even if he insisted on either of them having an arranged marriage, they wouldn't, they had been brought up in a very different England to the one that he had. They were in mainstream education and religion played a very small part of their lives. But they both had their parents' work ethic and not only helped in the shop, but were both at university. Kal was studying economics and Mena was wanting to be a teacher. They had so much more opportunity for education than he had and he envied them, especially Kal and the chance to study economics. He himself had left school with a handful of O Levels and had gone straight to work full-time in his parents' shop. But it had been a good education and by the time he had married Mani he had been running a shop of his own and had bought his current shop when the kids were little.

Mr Singh doubted that either of his children would follow into his footsteps and be full-time shopkeepers, and if the truth be known he wouldn't want them to, there were easier ways to make money, but he appreciated having them there for the time being. He had employed people before and he would do it again. It was just a case of finding the right people; he had learnt the hard way years earlier when he employed a series of employees who had thought nothing of helping themselves to stock or money from the till.

But he would sort something when the time came. There were plenty of people who came into the shop he wouldn't mind employing, that nice lady from the bookmakers included; she had an honest face and he knew she was a hard worker. She was probably on a much better wage where she was than the one he would be offering, but he wasn't going to worry about all of that now. He had enough on his plate to worry about with the shop without putting more worries in his head.

When he had first taken over the shop it had been exactly what it had said on the tin. It was a convenience store and people came in and shopped there because it was convenient, not caring that they were paying a few pence extra because the shop was on their doorstep. It thrived for those first few years and the family reaped the benefits, even building a small extension on the back so they could store stock and extend the shop so they could carry more lines. They sold lots of stuff, all the regular grocery-type stuff and of course seasonal lines – Easter, Christmas they had it all covered. They stocked greeting cards, newspapers and magazines, even a small collection of toys and household goods. If someone asked for something they would do their best to stock it. But then the big guns arrived in town and built a superstore less than a mile away from Singh's shop. It was open 24 hours a day; well, apart from Saturday and Sunday nights. Barring that, you could shop at all hours. And of course they sold everything – electrical goods, CDs, DVDs, clothes.

Suddenly his clientele were only coming into his shop for the odd bit stuff, daily newspapers, cigarettes, lottery and the other things they had either ran out of or had forgotten to get with their weekly shop. Ravi Singh was desperate. Every week the takings were down and he was at a loss as to how to begin to fight the supermarkets. He had almost given up.

But then there were his regular customers who didn't go to the supermarket. The ones that just shopped daily. What would they do if he threw the towel in? He spoke to other family members who had faced similar situations, they all told him the same thing. Hold in there.

And to a certain extent they were right. He had to adjust how he stocked the shop; he certainly didn't carry as much fresh stuff and what he did have he was quick to reduce the price of and sell before it became unsellable and he would have to destroy it, but if people asked for fresh meat he would get it for them and that seemed to work. He had put notices up all over the shop advertising the meats they could order for collection on a weekend and every Friday afternoon he would make the journey to a local meat wholesalers and collect his order. He would add little bit on for himself, but the profit wasn't the point; it was getting customers through the door and they in return were getting reasonably priced fresh meat.

Because it worked for the meat, he also did it for fish and he would take orders for big bags of potatoes; these he would even deliver to the customers' homes. It was a half-hour job, his customers lived in a five-mile radius of the shop.

So the shop evolved. He employed a paperboy; the more elderly didn't mind paying an extra pound or so a week for having their papers and magazines delivered. And then in one bad winter, he offered to deliver orders to customers who couldn't get out of their homes to come to him. As long as they rang before lunchtime, they would have their order by tea. It worked. Word got around and somehow it wasn't just in the bad weather people didn't mind paying a bit extra to have their orders delivered straight to their homes; it was now a regular service.

By listening and adapting, the shop was holding its own; nowhere near its heady days before the supermarket, but it was doing all right. His van was jam-packed every day with goods from the cash and carry and his meat, fish and potato orders were growing steadily each week. When the supermarket also started to do home delivery, he thought he was done for, but it had had little effect on his own business. People were used to him delivering, they liked what he sold and they were happy either ringing their orders in or handing him their shopping list when he dropped off their orders.

It was hard work for Mr Singh and his family. They worked long hours and seldom had time off. Mani would spend her days taking orders and then packing them up for delivery and Kal would either man the shop while his dad went out in the van or go himself. Mena would do what she could in the shop when she could; still in her first year at university, her time was precious.

He was proud that they had all pulled together and were keeping their heads above water. His dad thought he was mad; that they did too much, especially when he told him that he was known to let some of his customers tick on. He knew who would pay when they got some money and he knew who wouldn't. So the trustworthy ones were allowed to run a small account; nothing big, just up to £10, but it could mean the difference between a child going to school without breakfast, or there being no heating on because the gas had run out and they wouldn't have any money until the next day. It was horses for courses and Mr Singh knew his customers well. He would never let anyone go hungry.

These people lived in his community and the hard times they fell on weren't always of their own doing. He would do what he could to help with gas, electricity and food, but he drew the line at letting people buy cigarettes and alcohol on account; they weren't necessities; not in his eyes anyway. And he found by showing kindness, they would pay him back as soon as they could more than likely on the off chance that they might just need to run up a bill again. Whatever the reason they paid him back, it worked.

He also started a Christmas club, well, Mila did. Every week people would come and pay money in, Mila would write it into a big book with a running total so the customers always knew how much they had belonging to them and then at Christmas they could either have the money back in cash or they could buy goods to the value of their savings plus 10% more; it was a good business move. They would spend the money in the shop because they were getting the extra bit, but the Christmas club money was sometimes a necessity to Mr Singh when his cash flow hit a bump in the road, which it often did in the course of the year, and he would use it to help him out instead of going into his overdraft and paying a fortune for the privilege. It had been a very savvy business move his beautiful Mila had come up with. Happy shopkeepers and happy customers.

But there was a downside as well. Even though he had been born in this country people said cruel things about him. He paid his taxes and contributed to society, but some people thought he and his family were scum of the earth; young kids would open the door and shout abuse at him and many a time he would come down in a morning to find dog poo pushed through his letterbox. It was upsetting and hurtful. He tried to do his best for the community, but there was a minority who took offence at the colour of his skin, or the turban he wore. Sometimes when he refused credit to a drunk who wanted a bottle of vodka, the expletives would spew out of their mouths. He wouldn't show them it upset him, but it did and the words would ring around his head for days.

It was worse when the abuse was aimed at Mila or the kids; then he would get mad. But what could they do? They just had to take it and make a note who the troublemakers were for the future. Usually aggressors would be in the next day, when they had sobered up, apologising. He would accept the apology as politely as he could, but it made Mr Singh sad to think that they were the cause of all of the hatred just because of the colour of their skin or their religion. It was the same the whole world over though, he read about it every day in the newspapers he stocked. It was a very broken society and he didn't know how it could ever be fixed. So he kept his head down, had a ready smile and a kind word for his customers and hoped for a miracle that would never happen.

Saturday nights were always busy in the shop. Kal was helping out, but it was still a bit frantic. Firstly it would be the lottery, then it would be a steady queue for alcohol and cigarettes with the odd scratch card thrown in. At each lull, he would add to the ever growing list of things he needed to get from the cash and carry first thing on Monday morning. It would be a jam-packed van as usual, but that meant that business had been good over the weekend so he mustn't grumble.

He saw Susan come in; she was a regular and was one of the few he knew by name. She always came in on a Saturday night and always bought the same things. She came in other days as well, but that was usually for groceries, Saturday it was always wine. She was a pleasant woman and would chat away as Mr Singh wrapped the wine and put it into carrier bags. From what he could make out she cared for her elderly mother, but beyond that he knew little; he didn't even know if there was a Mr Susan, she always came in alone and on a Saturday she always bought three bottles of his special offers on wine for £10.

Tonight was no different. She chatted about the weather as he wrapped each bottle of wine in tissue paper and placed them carefully in a carrier bag. 'Yes the weather had been cold, no there was no sign of spring!' She handed him a £20 note and he took £10, HE75 229564, off the top of the pile of £10 notes in his till. With a pleasant goodnight, she was out of the door and away. He did wonder if the wine was all for her. Perhaps she did have a husband at home to share it with, he didn't like to think of her drinking alone.

But he couldn't dwell too much on her, if he started to worry about his customers he would never sleep at night. Times were hard for everyone whether it be money, health, stress or just loneliness. He couldn't do much to help, but he made a concerted effort to buy things from the cash and carry that were on special offer or were price marked as a bargain. And he always tried to pass on the savings to his customers. It was never much; a penny here or a penny there. But his philosophy had always been 'look after the pennies and the pounds will look after themselves'. Every little would help. The door opened and a crowd of young girls came into the shop; he turned his head and studied the CCTV to see what they were up to, because he knew of old that given the chance they'd be trouble.

6

Worth Your Weight in Gold

Susan Cole let herself into the house. It was cold and dark. It wasn't the weather for leaving the heating off, but she had been out all day and had forgot to knock the heating onto timed; usually she had it timed to come on mid-evening so by the time she got home the chill would be out of the rooms.

As it was, she would have to keep her coat on for the next half-hour or so, but it was something she did often, the heating timer was usually one of the last things on her mind. Making straight for the kitchen, she opened a cupboard and took herself a glass out. Unwrapping one of the bottles, she filled the glass almost to the top and took herself a huge gulp. She had had the day from hell, her nerves were shot and her body ached from top to bottom. The plan was she would have herself this glass of wine and when the house had warmed through she would have a soak in the bath and by that time it would be probably time for bed. Tomorrow would be here before she knew it and it would start all over again. She took another big gulp of her wine and refilled the glass.

While she waited for the heating to start to have some effect, she picked up her post and went to draw the curtains in the living room. It was all neat and tidy just as she had left it that morning. There was only her living there so there was seldom a thing out of place; she always dusted and hoovered before she left on a morning. She hated the thought of returning home late and having to start on her housework, not that there was ever much to do, the house was small and she didn't make much mess, it was just dust really. But she liked to keep the house tidy. *'A tidy house is a tidy mind!' Isn't that a saying?* she thought to herself.

Her mind wasn't tidy though, it hadn't been for a while now. The wine helped. It seemed to slow it down and stop it from spinning so much, then she could sleep soundly instead of lying in her big double bed thinking for hours and hours. The wine was a new thing, well, not new entirely, maybe for the past couple of years, but it seemed to take more and more for the wine to kick in and the thinking to stop. She had it under control though, it wasn't a problem.

Susan Cole had been a widow for the past 20 years. Widowed at 32, she had never really got over the shock of losing Arnie so suddenly. They had only been married ten years, he had gone out to work one day and never came back. It had been his heart, they said; he had been dead before he even hit the ground, it had been that quick. But it was a cruel way to go; especially for Susan. She felt cheated and robbed and to some effect she died as well when Arnie did; her life would never be the same again. She had gone through the motions of the funeral and the months that followed on some kind of auto-pilot. It felt like she was a bystander, she had no emotions. There was no weeping or wailing and everyone who knew her said she was coping beautifully. But they didn't know. They didn't know her really. They saw what they wanted to see, they saw what Susan wanted to show them.

No one saw how she was behind closed doors. They didn't see her crawling the walls in desperation or hear the wailing that went with it. 'It's tragic!' they would say. 'But you're young and you'll meet someone else. Arnie wouldn't want you to be on your own!' She didn't want anyone else, she wanted Arnie. He had been her best friend; her soulmate. They had had a good marriage. Even when children didn't materialise it hadn't been the end of the world; they had each other. They both worked hard, they had a little house they both loved and they took lovely holidays, happily seeing different parts of the world together.

It didn't matter that they didn't have children. It didn't until Arnie died and then it meant a lot. Susan had nothing left of Arnie. That was when it hit her that maybe they should have tried harder to have a baby, maybe they should have had it investigated instead of thinking it was just the way it was; that they were just meant to have each other. It was all so cruel. The pain she felt was almost tangible.

The passing of time didn't particularly help. People expected her to be coping better so that was what she showed them. She would see family and meet up with friends, carry on working and she would put on a show. Yes she was fine. Blah, blah, blah. But she felt no different, her heart had stopped when Arnie's had and it showed no sign of restarting. The wardrobe in her bedroom was testament to her grief; some of his clothes still hung there. Behind closed doors she was still the grieving widow. She talked out loud to him just as she would have done if he had still been there. She watched things on the television that she knew he would have enjoyed watching with her. In the privacy of her home, Arnie was very much alive.

It had been a long twenty years; in the beginning she had thought about following him, but then she had always thought that people who did away with themselves ended up in purgatory, somewhere she knew Arnie wouldn't be. If she thought of where Arnie was it was somewhere pretty with a little river where he would sit for hours with his flask and sandwiches and fish. Just like he had done when he was alive. That wasn't purgatory, that was Arnie's idea of heaven. So what happened if she went to join him and ended up somewhere completely different? She couldn't take the chance, so would bide her time. She would live this thing that was her life and she would wait her turn. When the time was right and her number was called she would see him again. If she was good, that was. And recently she didn't always feel good. Thanks mainly to Betty. Betty Cole; Arnie's mother!

She had Alzheimer's or at least the onset. She had been on a steady decline for the past three years, but for the past six months she had been quite poorly. That wasn't the right word, she wasn't poorly as such; she was as strong as an ox, apart from her mind that wandered and confused her. It was a sorry sight. But Susan was all she had. Both her sons had passed before her and her other daughter-in-law had remarried years earlier and her total correspondence to Betty was flowers on birthdays, Mother's Day and Christmas; Susan hadn't had sight of her since Arnie's funeral. So when the confusion started, it was Susan that went to the rescue; Arnie would have wanted her to and to be honest she wouldn't have it any other way.

But now Betty was consuming her whole life. Today for instance, she had been there all morning, then had had to rush into town because she needed to order her a bed before the shops closed and then she had gone back and not left until just after 8 o'clock. She had fed her, tidied around, washed and ironed, been shouted at, cried at and then loved. Sometimes Betty knew who she was, sometimes she thought she was her neighbour, more often than not she thought she was a stranger and that's when it got really hard.

Betty's grip on reality was becoming less and less. Susan was having to lock her into the house when she left just in case she wandered out and got lost. She couldn't bear the thought of Betty wandering the streets around her home not knowing where she lived or who she was. A neighbour had a spare key in case of an emergency, but it wasn't good enough. What if Susan was run over by a bus on her way home? Who would care for Betty then? Who would even know to go and check on her? Maybe her neighbour, but that might take days and by then Betty could have done herself some serious damage.

As it was, Susan had to make sure that there was nothing left lying around that Betty could get her hands on. Tonight she had left a flask of warm tea — not scalding in case she spilt it on herself, sandwiches wrapped in foil and some biscuits. There were chocolates and a bottle of pop beside her bed in case she woke in the night hungry; at least if she had her chocolates and lemonade she would resist the urge to get out of bed and rummage around in the kitchen and try and cook herself something. She had already arrived some mornings to exploded boiled eggs, charred toast and ovens left on all night. And that wasn't the half of it. Betty really was becoming a threat to herself.

Susan had always kept in touch with Betty; even in her darkest hours after Arnie had died, she would go and see his mam. She had lost Arnie too and if anyone had an inkling how Susan was feeling, it was Betty. The funny thing was that before Arnie went they hadn't been particularly close, Susan would even make excuses not to go and see her with Arnie, she found Betty a bit of a cold fish. But then Arnie went and she found herself drawn to Betty like a magnet and a strange sort of companionship took shape.

They would go out for Sunday lunch together or to the theatre, they had even had a few weekends away together. Whatever they were doing, Susan always made sure that she saw Betty at least a couple of times a week and called her on the telephone almost daily. Like Susan, she had been a widow for a long time too, worse for her even, she had lost her two sons too. But she was much more a glass half full type and thought she had been blessed for the time she had had with each of the men in her life. 'Life is for the living, Susan!' she would say when Susan was having a particularly bad day. She would agree, the mask would slide back into place and it would stay there until she reached the comfort of her own four walls and then the weeping and wailing would start.

So when she noticed that Betty wasn't quite herself, she was concerned and took her off to the doctors. Tests were done, but there was nothing untoward and they only had to go back if things deteriorated. Of course they did; nothing drastic, just small things that set alarm bells ringing in Susan's head. Betty was 78; she might not have looked it but she was definitely slowing down significantly and she seemed to get confused about the simplest things. Back at the doctors, more tests, then a referral to hospital and a diagnosis of early Alzheimer's and some literature for Susan to read.

It was all horrific, poor Betty. Susan upped her visits, helped with the housework and always made sure that any food in the house was in date and safe for Betty to eat. They would go for walks and she would take her shopping and out for meals. She read that doing puzzles helped so they would spend evenings playing Scrabble and doing crosswords together. Whatever kept Betty sharp they attempted and it seemed to work. There were times when she was confused, but they were few and far between, at least when Susan was with her. But then about six months ago she somehow managed to lock herself in her bathroom. Luckily it was a Friday and Susan always called first thing on a Saturday morning either to take Betty shopping or if she didn't think she was up to it, make a list and go and do it herself.

When she heard Betty talking to herself upstairs she thought nothing of it, shouting up to let Betty know she was there. She was shocked when she started banging on the bathroom door. Thinking she had had a fall Susan raced up the stairs and into the bathroom. The door hadn't been locked at all, Betty had forgot how to open it. The sight before Susan made her cry. It was obvious she had been in the bathroom all night; she had wet herself even though she was actually sitting next to the toilet and she had took great big bites out of the soap and not knowing if she had forgot how to turn the taps on or had forgot that there was actually water in the taps, Betty had been drinking shampoo and bubble bath.

Betty cried when she saw Susan. The two women sat on the bathroom floor holding each other and sobbed. It was the beginning of the end for Betty. Susan rang for an ambulance, unsure what else Betty had eaten or drank. Luckily the bleach still seemed to be intact with its child lock proving too much for a confused Betty. She ended up spending two weeks in hospital while they assessed her. When Susan went in for a meeting with her care team they were sympathetic, but the only local care home that could deal with Betty's condition didn't have a bed; she would be put on the waiting list, but her condition wasn't as severe as some and to be honest sometimes just being able to live in their own homes proved to be better for them than being in strange places with strange people.

Susan worked full-time at the police headquarters. That was where she had met Arnie years earlier; she had worked in the office and he was a young police constable. When he died they had been amazing and let her have as much time off as she needed and then when she was ready, to return to work part-time until she felt able to go back full-time. She knew when she left the hospital after the meeting that she was going to have to ask if she could work part-time again if she was going to help look after Betty. It would be impossible to work her normal hours and then go to her mother-in-law's before and after work. She couldn't see it being a problem; she had been a good and loyal employee and the only time she had any length of time off was when she lost Arnie.

Money wouldn't be a problem either. Her house had been paid for and because Arnie had died in service she had got a lump sum and had his pension. She earned good money with her job and she didn't spend much on herself. Apart from work clothes and her regular haircut, that was it really. So there was really no reason for her not to do it, she wanted to do it, but with no idea how long it would be for she had to agree to a one-year contract on part-time hours, signing it filled her with dread. What if Betty went into a home in a matter of weeks? What would she do with all of that extra time on her hands? It was a problem she never got to face.

Before Betty came home, she readied the house for her arrival. She removed all items that she deemed dangerous. Her dangerous and what Betty was capable of making dangerous were two very different things. At first it all worked out fine. She didn't need to start work until 10am so she would leave her own house at 8am and make straight for her mother-in-law's. She would help her dress and make her breakfast and leave her a sandwich for her lunch. Leaving work at 2.30pm she would reverse the journey and at Betty's she would do any housework that needed doing, give her tea and leave her a little something for her supper. Before she left she would either help Betty bathe or just get her ready for bed. She would leave at about 8pm and make her way back to her own home and update Arnie on the day's events while she made herself a snack and settled herself in for the night.

At first it worked beautifully, Betty was bright and content and seemed to have forgotten all about her ordeal in the bathroom. But then the odd thing started to happen, the eggs, the toaster, she even put the electric kettle onto the gas ring to boil it and made an almighty mess of it. Every day she had to carry out a series of risk assessments and found herself doing more and more. The house was starting to smell because she daren't open the door to let air in or Betty would be off and if she left the windows open Betty would have a dickey fit thinking that the birds that tweeted away in her garden would get in, or moths or spiders or burglars and so it went on.

Every day brought a new challenge. Susan rang Social Services for help, but there was none forthcoming, it seemed that by all accounts Betty's doctor was happy with the care she was receiving from her daughter-in-law and her name remained on the list as a non-priority. There were carers who came in a couple of times a day, but even though all of the ladies that came were lovely, Betty was having none of it and had even chased one of them with a pair of scissors; something else that Susan had overlooked and needed to have removed. So in the end it was just Susan.

Betty's mind came and went. When sometimes Betty reverted to childhood or when she didn't know who Susan was it would break Susan's heart. She started to spend more and more time in her other world and sometimes she would scream at Susan to get out of her house. On a couple of occasions Susan had actually had to go and hide upstairs for an hour or so until Betty stopped ranting; when all was quiet she would make her way back downstairs to be greeted like a long-lost friend.

She was starting to become a danger to herself and to others. It was hard work and the constant worry had started to take its toll on Susan. Always fond of a glass of wine with a meal, something that her and Arnie had always enjoyed and something she had continued doing even when she lived on her own, now she found that the minute she set foot in her door after a day at work and with Betty, instead of making herself a nice cup of coffee like she would normally have done, now she was pouring herself a glass of wine before she had even taken her coat off.

Her nerves were shot and the insomnia she had suffered on and off for years was back with a vengeance. The wine helped; she would find herself quite relaxed before she got into her bed but when she found that one glass wasn't enough, she had poured herself another. And so the pattern had continued. Now she found herself stopping at the shop at least three nights a week to buy her three bottles of wine.

She never thought that she actually got drunk, she was just less stressed, a bit more relaxed. Well, sometimes; other times the drink would make her feel very sorry for herself and she would find herself ranting at Arnie, who always seemed to be sitting in his armchair when she had a little drink. She would shout and scream and call him names; on a couple of occasions she had actually thrown things at him. But he was the same old Arnie as ever and never retaliated; just sat there and took it and waited for Susan to get it out of her system. She would make her way upstairs in a strop. 'Bugger you, Arnie Cole, you can sleep down there in your armchair, you're not getting into my bed!' She would fall into her bed, usually fully dressed, and sleep until morning. But there would be no Arnie in the armchair in the cold light of day and the sorrow would wash over her afresh.

Susan knew she needed help; she need help with the ever unpredictable Betty and she needed help for herself. Her drinking was getting silly; she was a middle-aged lush, because whether she wanted to believe it or not, every day she looked for a drink and that wasn't normal behaviour. She wasn't coping at all. At work she was finding it hard to concentrate; she made mistakes and had been pulled on a couple of occasions because of it. She had been mortified; always the professional, she didn't make mistakes. She blamed the pressures of home life, but she knew it was more than likely because of her hangover that every day seemed to take longer and longer to clear.

When Betty started to dirty her bed, Susan didn't know what to do. She put black plastic bin bag liners between the mattress and the sheets, but they would crinkle and rustle and Betty complained about them constantly. She bought special protectors which seemed to help, but the bed was ruined and even though she had washed it down a hundred times the stains wouldn't lift. And then there was the washing; it wasn't just night times that Betty would forget to go, it seemed that apart from when she really wanted to go, she didn't bother going for the smaller stuff at all and would just wee away at her leisure.

It needed drastic action. The doctor had been called back in and now he agreed that maybe Betty needed around-the-clock care, but presently there was still no room. He suggested incontinence knickers in the short term, maybe try again with the carers and perhaps if she sold her home there may be provision somewhere else, but she would have to pay for it. Susan was in wholehearted agreement; Betty was getting too much for her and she had the bruises to prove it. She really didn't know how much longer she could go on, it was having such an effect on her own life. Not that she had much of a one, but the drinking alone was cause for concern.

There would be plenty of money to keep Betty for as long as she needed caring for; one, three, five or even ten years. It was an old Victorian house in a sought-after part of the town. Even though it needed a facelift, structurally it was sound and it would sell at a good price. Susan as Betty's executor took matters into her own hands and placed the house on the market. It proved to be a little bit more complicated than she had envisaged; there was no way that Betty would cope with strangers walking around gawping at her and her home. So the estate agent had suggested that they would take a great number of photographs and if anyone wanted to see it they would just have to look from the outside. Obviously this had a detrimental effect on the price, but it was far better than risking Betty having one of her to-dos!'

But the house could take weeks to sell, at the worst

months. In the meantime Susan was just going to have to do her best and hope that a place would come up for Betty in the local home before the sale of the house. She had ordered a new bed and had had to virtually wrap Betty up in cotton wool to keep her safe. Susan herself was exhausted and frazzled. Thinking that Betty wouldn't appreciate the carers coming back in, Susan had declined, perhaps foolishly, so now the responsibility was all on her. Tempted as she was to make her life easier for herself by moving in with Betty albeit temporarily, so far she had resisted. She would miss Arnie and she would miss her wine.

Somehow she thought that the end was maybe in sight. Social Services agreed that Betty needed care and failing that, if the house sold, they would be able to look around for somewhere who would care for her privately. Susan would have a bit of her life back and in the process have a bit of the old Betty back.

Because that was half the problem with the drinking, this new, dirty, confused, silly old woman was starting to turn into the bane of Susan's life and she was starting to dislike her. She didn't like having the responsibility, she didn't like the constant running backwards and forwards to her house, the cooking the cleaning, the endless washing and ironing, of stripping and making beds, dressing and undressing Betty. She resented her more than she could have ever thought possible.

But then later, mellowed by the wine, she would hate herself for thinking like that.

Betty had been a good friend to her over the years; kind, generous, patient. She hadn't asked for any of this, she would be mortified if she had the smallest inkling what she was doing; she had always been such a private and proud lady. But then Susan would feel worse and another glass of wine would be poured. It was a vicious circle.

By the time she fell asleep that Saturday night, Susan had had the best of two and a half bottles of wine. She hadn't even made it to bed, no, she had decided that she would just sit on Arnie's knee in his armchair and snuggle. When she woke in the morning she was cold and stiff; her head throbbed and there was a horrible tinny taste in her mouth. She felt like she had been sick, but there was no sign of it anywhere. No sick, no sign of Arnie; just a couple of bottles of wine and an empty packet of crisps.

It was 7am; she drank a cup of coffee and swallowed down a couple of paracetamols. By the time she left for Betty's she was feeling a little bit better, though try as she might, she had no recollection of the night before beyond switching on the heating and having herself a drink. 'This wine thing really has to stop!' she chastised herself as she opened Betty's front door.

All was well. Betty was still in bed, but opened an eye when she saw Susan.

'Morning Susan!' Betty said with clarity. Susan sighed with relief; it was going to be a good morning. Betty seemed to be Betty which was good. It meant that she would be happy sitting watching Morning Worship on the telly and eating her breakfast. The new bed was being delivered this morning so Susan had loads to do. If Betty was calm and quiet she would get through it all at twice the pace.

And she was good and Susan did get her work done. By the time the delivery lads arrived, everything in Betty's room was ship shape and in Bristol fashion. Betty was even content to sit while the old bed was removed and the new one installed. The lads had done a grand job and even insisted that it was no bother dropping the old bed off at the tip.

Susan was so grateful; she really didn't know what she was going to do with the old smelly one. She had already paid for the bed and the delivery in the shop, but she felt like she needed to give the lads something for their trouble. Finding her purse, she fished around and found two £10 notes; HE75 229564 was one of them. Explaining that she was ever so grateful to them, she handed the lads a £10 note each and told them to have a couple of pints on her. They were delighted and as she waved them off at the door she felt it was £20 well spent.

Checking Betty was still happy sitting, she made her way upstairs and placing the protectors on first, re-made Betty's bed. Just the old one not being in the room did wonders for the odour and with a splash of air freshener, Susan made her way back downstairs to see what needed to be done next.

Lunch. Two mugs of milky coffee and a piece of chocolate cake each. She hadn't had time to do anything else, but she had put a little chicken in the oven and she would do some veg and Yorkshires and they would have it for their tea. Betty was watching Country File, it had always been another of her favourites and she seemed to be enjoying watching it. She started to tell Susan about Arnie and his brother Rob delivering a lamb when they were on a school outing as boys. It was a true story and one that both Arnie and Betty had told her many years earlier. Placing the coffee and cake down beside her, Betty reached over and took a great big bite and then another; her appetite was good that day. Sipping on her coffee she looked at Susan as if she was going to say something but then stopped herself.

'What is it, Betty?' Susan asked, sure that whatever the answer was going to be was going to be rubbish; she had been lucid for quite some time that day. 'I just wanted to say, Susan, I don't know what I would do without you. You've been better than any daughter I could ever have had. You're worth your weight in gold. Thank you!' Susan was stunned; she hadn't been expecting that. Suddenly all the emotions of the previous months came welling up and Susan found it difficult not to lose control. She grabbed Betty's hands and then cuddled her, all the time telling her it didn't matter, she loved her etc., etc.

When she had her emotions back under control she released herself from Betty's arms and leant back on her hunkers and looked up at her. She looked different; but she smiled at Susan again and said, 'Do you want to come out and play? My dad has made me some skipping rope…'

7

A Pretty Penny

illy the Kid ambled back to the delivery van grinning, the £10 note he had been given by the nice lady safely tucked away in his jeans pocket. He wasn't really called Billy; he was William and he wasn't a kid; he was almost 30. But he had had the nickname for as long as he could remember and he was used to it.

He was chuffed to bits with the tenner; it meant that he could see Cha Cha later and the grin on his face got even bigger. He often helped Kenny with deliveries on a weekend. Kenny would text him the night before he needed him and he was always happy to help. He had worked Saturday afternoon and Sunday morning this week; Kenny would be handing him over £40 when they finished today. They just had one more delivery to make and then a quick run to the tip to drop off the nice lady's smelly old mattress and then he would be dropped off at home where his mam would plate up his Sunday dinner while he had a shower.

At 29 he supposed he was a bit old still to be living at home. But like his mam said, he was special. He knew himself he wasn't like other lads his age; he wasn't even like his younger brother and sister; they had both left home years ago and now there was just William and his mam and dad. He liked living at home though; his mam was a brilliant cook and there was always lovely tea and his dad would sometimes let William help him in their huge garden. He had a nice room with a television and Sky and an Xbox with all the latest games, and he would enjoy beating his brother James when he came over to see them.

But he couldn't work properly. He had never had a job; he wasn't really sure why because he liked helping Kenny and wouldn't mind doing it every day. He wasn't allowed though and his mam had told him over and over, if anyone asked what he was doing out in Kenny's van he had to say he was just helping a friend and he wasn't getting paid. She said it so often to him that he couldn't possibly forget. *I'm helping a friend, I'm helping a friend, I'm helping a friend!* he would chant over and over again in his head as he sat in the passenger seat of the van next to Kenny.

He liked getting money of his own though and Kenny was always nice to him; if there was something heavy to carry Kenny would always tell him how to pick it up and put it down so he didn't hurt himself. And Kenny would always buy him a bacon sandwich and a Coke somewhere on their journey. He liked that bit too. It was fun and if it was work, then he liked it. His mam would give him pocket money, but that was just £5 here and there; anything he wanted she would get for him or go with him if it was a new game for his Xbox or something. His mam looked after him really well.

He had lots of friends. Most of them he had gone to primary school with or they had lived in his street so he would play with them when he got in from school. Now they were all older; most had moved away, but he would still see them in his local pub where he usually went on a Friday and Saturday night. He liked to play darts and dominoes and some of his friends were on his team. Most of them were married now and had children of their own, but they never forgot about Billy the Kid and he had lost count of the engagements, weddings and Christenings he had been to. He had never had a girlfriend of his own; apart from Cha Cha who wasn't really a girlfriend, but he loved her anyway.

William wasn't sure what was wrong with him. He had gone to primary school with the rest of his friends, but he always had someone helping him with his reading and writing. He liked sums but he wasn't very good at reading. When he was 11 he went to a different school to the rest of his friends. Every morning a minibus would come and collect him and take him to a school in a different part of town. He still did sums and writing, but there were other things to do, like playing on a computer or doing art. He liked that school; he had lots of friends there and was happy. When he finished school at 16 he went to college; again the minibus would come to collect him but now all he did was computers and he soon grew bored and started to get up to mischief. The college weren't happy and asked him to leave. He hadn't been or done anything since.

His days were filled with DVDs and Xbox games; sometimes he would go shopping with his mam or gardening with his dad when he got in from work. Sometimes he would help look after his niece and nephews, but he was never allowed to take them to the park or the shops on his own. His mam said it was in case he forgot them, but he wouldn't do that; he loved them.

Sometimes he would go to the cinema with his sister and brother-in-law, or his brother would take him to a football match. He never really got bored, he always seemed to have something to do. Even though he would have liked a full-time job like the one he had with Kenny, he really didn't know when he would have time to do it.

His dad always said he had been dropped on his head as a baby. The thought of anyone dropping him made William feel ill; who could have done such a thing to him? But his mam said his dad was just joking; he hadn't really been dropped. But that was sometimes his problem; he believed everything that everyone said to him, whether they were just joking or they were lying. He just couldn't tell, even when he watched their faces for the tell-tale smile, he didn't always get it.

But his mam had said that there had been some complications when he was born. It was something to do with a cord or something. Anyway whatever it was it had stopped him getting oxygen and some of his head didn't work properly. Sometimes he wondered what he would be if he hadn't hurt his head; would he be clever like his brother and sister? They were both very smart, but it didn't matter. He had the best time because he still lived with his mam and dad.

The next delivery was done, this time it had been

two sofas and even though they had carried the sofas into the living room and moved them around until the lady was happy with them, she wasn't as nice as the bed lady and she didn't give them any extra money. The tip was next to get rid of the smelly old mattress and then they were on their way back to William's house.

Kenny thanked him, handed him two crispy £20 notes and told him he would text him when he needed him next. William was hardly out of the van when Kenny sped away with a loud *toot toot* on his horn. Going into the house, he could smell the roast beef straightaway. Even though he had had a bacon sandwich just over an hour earlier, he was starving. 'Upstairs and shower and I'll plate your dinner. You stink, William!' his mam said, laughing and making her way into the kitchen to sort out the dinner that had been kept for William earlier.

He had a good shower; he scrubbed and scrubbed his skin, just in case the smell of the mattress had rubbed off onto him, and he washed his hair – twice. Changing into some clean clothes he went back downstairs just in time for his mam to put his dinner onto a tray so he could go and sit in the living room and watch the football with his dad while he ate. It had been a good day and it was going to get even better when he saw Cha Cha later on.

His mam was asking if Kenny had paid him okay. 'Yes, of course Mam; why wouldn't he?' he answered. His mam always asked. He thought she didn't like the thought of people taking advantage of him, but he wasn't that stupid, he was a big lad and Kenny knew not to diddle him and he had heard Kenny telling people that Billy was strong, cheap and always did what he was told. When he told his mam what he heard Kenny saying she was mad as a hatter.

William wolfed down his dinner, had seconds of Yorkshire puddings, potatoes and gravy, followed by home-made spotted dick and custard, and when his mam brought him his football mug full of sweet tea, he helped himself to a handful of chocolate digestives. He was a working lad and needed fuelling up. And then he fell asleep; he lay on the settee on the pretence of watching the second half of the football but was asleep and snoring like a lion within minutes. He stayed that way for three hours and when he woke up he was starving.

So after munching his way through a plateful of sandwiches with a bag of crisps and a piece of cake, all washed down with a glass full of Coke, he went upstairs to have his second shower of the day and get ready for his night out.

He always liked to look his best when he went to see Cha Cha. He picked his newest pair of jeans and a rugby shirt he had got from his sister for Christmas. He gelled his hair and sprayed himself with aftershave. Looking in the mirror, he was happy with the reflection that stared back at him; he might be a bit on the hefty side but he was tall so he never looked fat. 'Just well made,' his mam would say. Shouting bye to his mam and dad, he made the five-minute walk to his local.

The pub was packed; there had been a local football derby on that afternoon and the pub was still full of football supporters who had had to make do with watching it on the telly. He spotted a couple of lads he knew and after getting himself a pint he made his way over to where they were standing playing on a bandit. Pleased to see him, they spent the next half an hour telling William how they had been robbed and the referee was a wanker! William didn't particularly like football. He had been watching it earlier with his dad, but he had no idea what the score was even when he was watching it, it had all been over when he woke up and he didn't think to ask his dad about the result.

William had another pint and then decided it was time he got himself off into town. He said goodbye to his very drunken friends and left the pub. It would have been easier getting the bus or a taxi into town, but he decided that he would rather save his money and walk. It wasn't often he had a bit of cash on him and he was looking forward to the night ahead. Within half an hour he was in the town centre and striding towards his destination.

The Glass House was a gentlemen's club. William thought that was funny because there were never any gentlemen in the place, well, not gentlemen like he saw on the telly. It was full of lads on stag dos and birthday parties or just groups of lads out having a good time. There were lots of other blokes that just went by themselves, just like he was. He came here sometimes. He liked the girls; they were all very friendly and some of the other lads he met there were always keen for him to join them. He liked it there.

He liked to watch the girls dance and if he had any money he would always ask Cha Cha to dance for him in the little room. Cha Cha was his favourite; she was so friendly to him and so pretty. Even if he couldn't afford a private dance, she didn't seem to mind and always had a smile on her face for him and sometimes she would even come and sit at the bar with him and have a chat and a drink. He wasn't even shy with her; she was so friendly. But tonight he had the money to give her for a dance, thanks to the nice lady with the bed; and that made him very happy.

As he looked around the club he couldn't see her. She wasn't on any of the poles and she wasn't sitting at the bar or in any of the booths chatting to other men like she usually did. He thought about asking one of the other girls, but they weren't a patch on Cha Cha and the thought did go through his head just to keep the money in his pocket and come back another night when Cha Cha might be working.

He had never had a girlfriend before. He wasn't sure why not; he didn't even know how to get a one or what he should do with one if he did. He had seen films and had read books, but apart from Cha Cha, he hadn't been near a woman in that way let alone kissed one. It didn't seem to bother him; he didn't seem to have the 'urge'. He had often wanted to ask his mam. Was that one of the things that had gone wrong with him when he was born or dropped on the head, or was it because of the tablets his mam gave him every day? Whatever the reason, he had never had the courage to ask her.

Even when Cha Cha took him into the little room and danced for him he liked to look at her, but that was as far as it went. He liked her smell and he liked the way her skin shone and her hair flowed down her back. But that was all. He loved her as a person and she was the only woman, apart from his mam and his sister, that he had in his life.

And then she was sitting next to him. 'Are you okay, Billy? How's it going?' He was over the moon; he was just about to leave and then there she was. They chatted; he told her about doing some deliveries with Kenny. He felt sure she wouldn't tell anyone he had made a bit of extra money and she told him about work and who had been in. They had a drink together and as she went to leave he asked her if it would be possible for her to give him a private dance. He took his £10 out of his pocket and straightened it out on the bar.

Cha Cha smiled at him; he didn't often ask her for a dance and she seemed genuinely over the moon that he had asked her. She picked up the £10, HE75 229564, and slipped it into her boot. Taking William by the hand she led him to the back of the club where the small rooms for private dances were located.

Twenty minutes later William was back at the bar having one more drink before he made the walk home. He was a happy lad; it had been a good day. Cha Cha had been as beautiful and as friendly as ever and he had enjoyed the warmth of her body near him. What was it his dad used to say about Jill Dando, that poor lady who was murdered off the telly? He would say she was as Pretty as a Penny! That's what Cha Cha was, as Pretty as a Penny. It had been £10 well spent and an unexpected treat. Tomorrow he would be back playing on his Xbox and watching bad movies on television, but for tonight he felt like a man; a normal man.

He finished his drink and left the club. He almost skipped all of the way home. If he was lucky his mam wouldn't be in bed and he knew there would be leftovers from the Sunday dinner. Maybe she would fry them up and put a nice egg on top for him. He was starving.

8

Fool's Gold

Cha Cha was doing her fourth private dance of the night. She had only been at work an hour and she still had five left to work. Sundays were usually slow, but because the football had been on, the town was busy and there was a steady stream of punters coming through the door. Mostly they were drunk and quick to part with their money; what was £20 quid at the end of a day's drinking? But because they were drunk they were a handful and thought they could take liberties with the girls.

But none of the girls were daft. They knew how to handle themselves; they had all had to learn fast. But if things did get out of hand, the bouncers would be in like a shot and the offender would be taken off the premises. Big Mama was always watching; that's what the girls called her anyway. Mrs aptly named Glass, who would sit and watch the club on CCTV and make sure that no harm came to the girls and that none of the girls took extra for extras. If Mrs Glass thought any of the girls were on the game then they would be up in her office before they knew what was happening. Cha Cha had never thought of doing extras and she didn't mind that Mrs Glass watched her every move; it made it a safe place to work. But some of the girls had tried to get away with charging punters for a grope and they had paid the price for doing it. There would be one warning and then if it happened again they would be out on their neck. Lots of girls had come and gone in the two years or so that Cha Cha had worked at The Glass House.

She hadn't intended staying there that long, just a couple of months to pay a few debts off. But the money was easy and even though in the beginning she had looked for other jobs, none would give her as much money as she got now for the hours she worked. And if she was honest, she quite liked the attention she got. She liked the 'look but don't touch' policy; it made her feel powerful. She had something they wanted to see and they had to pay for the privilege. It was a heady mix; money and power.

Of course she wasn't really called Cha Cha. She was plain old Lindsey O'Brien; 23 years old and at university studying English Literature. She didn't even know why she had decided to call herself Cha Cha; maybe because she could Cha Cha really well thanks to all of the ballroom dancing lessons she had had as a child. She had hated them at the time, all her friends were doing disco and hip hop, but she had done ballet and ballroom at her mam's insistence. Little did she know then that all those hours of waltzes, tangos and pirouettes would stand her in good stead as a lap dancer; she could certainly cut some moves and was certainly a hit with some of the regulars.

In her final year of university, she would be giving

the club up soon to concentrate on her finals; she wasn't going to take the chance of blowing it just so she could make a bit of money, she had worked too hard to do that. But where her fellow students struggled to make ends meet on their paltry grants, she always had cash to spare and had even built herself up a bit of a nest egg. But there was a price to pay and she kicked herself for letting it happen.

She had lived away from her parents' home since she was 16, firstly moving in with a friend whilst she went to college and them moving away from her home town to go to university. Her parents had no idea what her part-time job was, they were just impressed that she wasn't ringing them every five minutes for money like their friends' children did. There was really no reason that they should need to know; she would be moving on once she finished her degree anyway and The Glass House part of her life would be over, she just hoped that everything else was so easy to leave behind.

Sharing a house with four other students, they all knew what she did to make money in the wee hours. Often they would pop in and see her at the end of a night out and she liked the look on their faces when they saw her dangling off a pole wearing hardly any clothes. Cha Cha was very different from Lindsey. Cha Cha was all front and balls, whereas Lindsey was quiet and could even be described as shy and studious. They would sit in a booth, drink drinks from the bar using Cha Cha's discount and watch her work. Everything about Cha Cha was fake; fake tan, fake hair and so much make-up she was virtually unrecognisable to her peers. Lindsey wore hardly any make-up, even the fake tan would be scrubbed off her skin; her hair extensions would be brushed and left in her bedroom and her shoulder-length bobbed hair would be tied up in a ponytail. She was just very normal.

She enjoyed her studies; well, she had until her final year. Now she was struggling, there was just so much work to get through and not enough hours to get it done in. Even if she wasn't working she doubted if she would get much more done, but she really did need to think about leaving The Glass House before she lost sight of the finish line altogether. Some nights it would be almost 5am when she got in. By the time she got herself sorted it would be 6am and if she had an early lecture she would be dragging her backside back out of bed after only a couple of hours' sleep. Lindsey did try to keep on top of her timetable. She would try and leave the club early if she had an early lecture, but if it was busy Mrs Glass would huff and puff and in the end she would stay until the last punter had parted with his money.

She liked Mrs Glass; she had always been good to Cha Cha and when she had arrived there as plain old Lindsey Mrs Glass had seen some potential in her and had help evolve Lindsey into Cha Cha. The Glass House was the only club of its type in the town, but there were others in the city centre, so Mrs Glass was always on the lookout for ways to keep the punters coming through the doors and stop them going anywhere else. It was Cha Cha who she would always ask for advice or run ideas past. They had built up a good friendship over the years and Lindsey knew that Mrs Glass would pull out all the stops to keep her there. She was even known to turn a blind eye when

Cha Cha undercharged someone like she had earlier in the evening. Mrs Glass and her beady little eye would have seen that she had only taken £10 off that Billy lad. He must have forgotten that it was £20 for each dance, but she hadn't the heart to take another note off him. It wasn't as if she needed to do much for the money. Billy would be happy just sitting in a room holding her hand if she let him, the poor lamb. She often wondered if he wasn't quite right!

But lap dancing wasn't a career, it was a stop gap and a way to make some quick money. None of the girls stayed long, three or four years at most, and there were only a couple of girls over 40, but they were fit and could give the younger ones a run for their money. In fact both ladies were really popular, especially with the younger lads that came in; they were like bees around the honey pot and on weeks like Freshers' Week both ladies worked every night and made a small fortune. There was definitely something very appealing about the older woman.

Lindsey had set her heart on moving to London and doing her teacher training. She had friends who had put down roots there and she had decided that was the place to be when she finished her degree. She had applied to various schools in the London area and it would be a waiting game when she graduated, but as determined as ever, she would do it. This would all be a distant memory this time next year. But hand on heart she would miss everyone. The girls all watched out for each other and although unsure at first, she had grown to love their northern humour.

Apart from the punters and a couple of her housemates, there was no man in Lindsey's life. When she had first arrived at university she had had a torrid but short thing with a fellow student. It had been too fast and too intense and it had burnt out all too quickly; it had hurt. And from then on in she had been guarded around men; she didn't want to risk getting hurt again so didn't let anyone near her. That was another reason why she liked The Glass House so much, lots of attention with very little interaction. She was too busy to feel lonely or unloved and her bed certainly didn't feel too big for her; she was usually too exhausted even to think of the place beside her being empty.

And of course then there was her job. She might look like everyman's fantasy, but the truth of it was, would any bloke want their girlfriend gyrating around for other men? She thought not. And even though not many people knew what she did for her living, especially at university, she didn't want to risk getting involved with someone only to be dumped when they found out about Cha Cha.

Her alter ego was so far removed from her university persona that even her lecturers hadn't recognised her. One night a group of them had come in for a stag party; considering she had sat in a lecture with one of them only that afternoon, she was sure they would recognise her and she had a bit of a panic. But as the lecturer in question handed over his £20 note, he had no idea that little Lindsey O'Brien who he had advised earlier in the day about a piece of coursework she was struggling with, was also Cha Cha, the tall brunette wearing a thong and little else and who would be gyrating all over his knee in a matter of minutes. It was intoxicating.

The only time she had a break was when she went home in the holidays. Her mum and dad must have thought she worked and partied hard because for the first day or so back in her old bed, she slept. Lindsey was their only child and she had been brought up by a series of child-minders and after-school clubs. Both her parents were professionals so in the holidays she would be farmed out to one or other of her grandparents' houses for the duration and would return in time to go back to school. She loved them dearly, but she didn't really know them. Her dad was a chemist and worked for a large pharmaceutical company; her mum was a solicitor. Lindsey had come along late in their lives and had been a huge shock to them both. They were well established in both their careers and social lives and the arrival of a screaming baby girl had totally taken the wind out of their sails. So much so that her mum's mum and dad had had to move in for the first few years of Lindsey's life.

But they had got used to her and treated her as if she was made out of glass. They wanted nothing but the best for her, best school, best after-school activities. The pressure on Lindsey was enormous. So much so that by the time she had finished her GCSEs she had had enough and had moved in with her best friend. Her mum and dad had been devastated, they had thought that they had failed as parents. When Lindsey's results had arrived and she had got straight A's across the board they rethought the situation and decided that yes, it was maybe for the best and continued on with their jobs and upped their social life commitments.

They had a strange old relationship. They were

proud of Lindsey and her independence and were never shy about telling all their friends what a well-rounded individual Lindsey was. She often felt like she was some sort of trophy to be polished and placed on show whenever someone came around. But they didn't know the half of it and she wondered if what she was doing now was a form of rebellion against her parents and their middle-class ways. Especially Cha Cha; she knew without a shadow of a doubt that they would blow a gasket if they knew how she was funding her way through university. She hadn't really needed to do it, her mum and dad were always generous and would have happily given her a monthly allowance if she had asked. But she didn't want to; she wanted to be independent of them; she wanted to do it for herself. The less she was dependent on them the less chance she would end up like them. They weren't bad people; they were just what they were and Lindsey had no wish to end up in middle-class suburbia with them.

So she had Cha Cha and Cha Cha gave Lindsey a more common edge; she was an education all in herself and the lessons she had learned strutting her stuff in The Glass House were invaluable and would no doubt help her when she went forward with her life. She saw people now. She saw the girls that worked there; why they were there and the price they were paying for being there. And she saw the men. She could spot the married ones, the lonely ones, the letches; she would see them come in and before they had even uttered a word to her, she had them sussed.

Even Mrs Glass; Linda. She knew why she had set the club up and the reasons behind her. She was a lesson all in herself and Lindsey took on board what she heard. Mrs Glass was a sassy businesswoman, but she hadn't always been one. In her younger days she had been a stripper, doing the circuits of the local social clubs; it was a job she had to do to put food on the table when her husband was frequently in and out of work. By taking her clothes off for a room full of men she found that she could make more money on a Sunday lunchtime than she could be doing in any other type of job the rest of the week. Eventually she was in a position to stop, but when lap-dancing clubs started popping up all over the city, she jumped on the bandwagon and opened The Glass House.

It hadn't been an easy thing for her to do; she had had to beg, borrow and steal money, but she had done it and now The Glass House had a reputable reputation, if there was such a thing for such clubs. It was profitable, the girls liked working there because they were safe, something that Linda strived to do after the years of bad treatment on the stripping circuit, and she wasn't having her girls put at risk. Paying better wages than most, the girls were happy and happy girls meant happy punters and happy punters spent not only money on the girls, but money at the bar. So The Glass House was a university all on its own.

Going home was nice though, at least for a little while anyway. Lindsay never stayed as long as she intended to, she would be forever cutting her visit short and shooting off to see one of her friends in London or Manchester. As sad as it made her, there was only so much of her mum and dad she could take. Both sets of grandparents had passed on, all at a grand old age, and with no other relatives that she knew well enough to visit, she would make an excuse to go and see a friend before making her way back to university and The Glass House. It didn't seem to bother her mum and dad; by that time they would have had a good catch-up, meals out and drinks in, but with Lindsey being home they would feel obliged to come home from work early to see her and with both of them their jobs had always come first. Lindsey always felt like they each had a sigh of relief when she left and they could get back to normality.

Sunday night in the club continued at a pace. The bar was packed and on occasions Cha Cha had to wait for a little room to become vacant so she could take a gentleman inside for one of her private dances. Mrs Glass would be pleased. But it would be a late finish and Lindsey had some work she needed to finish and hand in to her tutor in the morning. It looked like she was going to have a sleepless night. But with a bundle of cash already stuffed in her thigh high boot, the night would be worth it; she hadn't had a drink and if she had a little pick-me-up before she got home then it would be fine.

As the night came to an end and the club started to clear down, she made a quick telephone call and booked herself a taxi home. She didn't always get a taxi, but she knew that Mark was working and he always looked after her. It was 3.45am before she had chance to cash up and then go and collect her belongings. It turned out that she was working the following night too; she had thought she had the night off, but Mrs Glass had put on a promotion and had took it as read that Cha Cha would want to work. She agreed to, but she did wonder when she would manage to get any sleep in the next 24 hours; she had coursework and lectures morning and afternoon. She might get a few hours before she returned to The Glass House but that would depend on what notes she had to write up or what other work the lectures produced. She knew for sure that she had to make a start on a book, *Confessions of an English Opium Eater*. Maybe she would bring it to work with her later and read it in her breaks, or maybe not! The title alone made her think that the book would need her undivided attention.

Mark was waiting outside The Glass Club in his taxi. She was still dressed for work which she could do if she taxied home; she would never dream of walking the streets as Cha Cha. She liked Mark, he had picked her up quite a bit recently and as they made the 10-minute journey back to her house, they always chatted away. He had recently become a father and was now working most nights to provide for his young family. He only knew Lindsey as Cha Cha; he had never seen her as herself and had the feeling that even though he would think he knew her quite well, if it happened he would walk past her in the street.

It was Mark who said he could help when she complained one night that she was dog tired but had coursework to do and then an early morning lecture. He said he had a little something that would pick her up, give her a bit of energy and enable her to concentrate. Harmless, he had said. £5 each and the effect could last up to 12 hours and there were no side effects. So she had agreed and had handed over her £5 and taken the little yellow pill as soon as she had got home from the club. And then she had worked and worked like she had never worked before. She flew through her assignment and finished off another piece of work that she had been neglecting for months and when it was a decent hour she had got the hoover out and done the house from top to bottom; much to her housemates' annoyance. And then off to lectures where she hadn't sat yawning throughout the monologue, but had taken very detailed notes. Her whole day had been a success and she felt completely normal. She slept as usual that night and woke as fresh as a daisy.

So the next time she saw Mark she handed him £10 and put the little tablets into her make-up bag just in case. But of course she did need them and the next time she spent £20. University was hard enough but with all of the late nights at The Glass House she needed the little yellow pills more and more. They were what she needed to get her to the end of her course. They helped her concentrate and they helped her dance her way through the night. But whereas one tablet now and then had little effect on her health, two was a cause for concern.

Sleep became a problem; she just didn't need it and when she did sleep she would have horrific nightmares. Her appetite was almost non-existent and she would have to force food down her. She was constantly thirsty and the inside of her mouth was always sore and bleeding because she chewed at it constantly. But she couldn't be without them. They were what got her through the days and before she knew it she was spending about £100 each week, which caused a bad situation to get worse because instead of working two or three nights she was now working five and buying more and more tablets just so she could keep one foot going in front of the other.

The weight was dropping off her; she had always been a little bit curvaceous, but now she could see herself that the curves were going; even her boobs were shrinking and Mrs Glass had commented on her new lithe figure. Cha Cha had shrugged it off saying it was just the stress of the finals coming. But realistically she knew she was in trouble and needed to do something about it.

Parked outside her house, she handed Mark his taxi fare. She was adamant that she wasn't going to buy any pills, but then she thought of the forthcoming day; the coursework; the reading; another night in the club and before she knew it she was back in her purse and handing over a further two £10 notes; one of them being HE75 229564. Mark took the money and delved under his seat for the first aid kit that he kept his supplies in. Closing the bag, he handed Cha Cha her tablets. 'Go easy with these, Cha Cha, Fool's Gold is just meant to be used now and again; you're popping them like Smarties!' Mark went on. Taking the tablets, she was out of the taxi and walking into the house; there was just so much she had to do!!!

9

In for a Penny, in for a Pound

Mark watched Cha Cha walk up to her house; already she was swigging on a bottle of water so no doubt she had taken one of the tablets. Cha Cha was a bit of an enigma to him; she looked like every other girl working at The Glass House, but when she opened her mouth and she spoke you would think she had been brought up with a silver spoon in her mouth. And she was smart; she was doing something really brainy at university. But she was a fool, and as much as it pained him to think it of her she was an addict.

He had never meant to cause Cha Cha any harm; he had only been trying to help and because she had always come across smart he thought she would know that somewhere along the line she would become hooked on the little pills. She hadn't though and her addiction to them was starting to take a toll on her; already he could see she had lost weight and he was certain that she was wearing twice as much make up as she used to. But it wasn't his problem. He couldn't counsel and advise everyone he sold gear to. He had enough problems of his own to worry about.

Mark Dickens had been taxiing for the past two and a half years. He had unexpectedly been made redundant soon after coming out of his electrician apprenticeship and resisting the urge just to blow his meagre redundancy, he had obtained his Hackney Licence and bought himself a car. But it was a hard trade. He would be working most nights and although he was attached to one of the local taxi firms, theoretically he was self-employed.

When his girlfriend of three months announced she was two months pregnant he almost ran for the hills. He liked Anna, but he didn't think for one minute that he loved her; he didn't really know her. She had been a fare he had picked up from the city centre one night and he had cheekily given her his mobile number. She had texted him the following day and they had met up for drinks, one thing led to another and he found himself regularly stumbling into her bed when he had finished a night on the taxi. The baby news took the wind right out of his sails; he was only 24 and the thought of providing for a baby terrified him; he could barely scrape a living to look after himself.

But Anna was adamant that she was keeping the baby; with or without him. So it would be with him; he wasn't a bastard and even if things didn't work out for him and Anna, he would be there for his baby. He moved into her little one-bedroomed flat and made the best of a bad job. To be honest they hardly saw each other, she worked days in a leisure centre and he worked nights on the taxi. He would get into bed as she was getting out. They would have a few hours on an evening before he went back to work and she went to bed. They muddled through. But money was tight; the rent on the little flat was astronomical because it was in the town centre; how she had managed it on her own puzzled Mark. There were two wages coming in and they had nothing to spare at the end of the month. But then she hadn't been buying baby stuff then. For such little things, they certainly needed some equipment and none of it was cheap.

The taxi bored him. Having always worked regular hours in a factory since leaving school, he found the whole sitting around waiting for fares soul destroying. Sometimes he could be sitting over an hour waiting for a fare to come in; often he would think about calling it a day for the night, but then what if a good fare came in? He would kick himself. So he would sit, sometimes in the taxi office, where the other 'cabbies' would regale each other about who they had had in their cars. Mark found it boring; who did they think they were? So usually he would sit in his car and read the paper or listen to the radio until something came in and he had something to do.

All in all, he wasn't happy with his lot. He hated his job, he had a girlfriend he didn't really know but had committed himself to. The only ray of sunshine on his horizon had been the baby, who for some unknown reason he was really excited about arriving. When they found out that it was actually a girl, he couldn't have been happier. All of a sudden as excited as he had been before they knew the sex, now he had a reason to get though the long nights on the taxi and take the money home for Anna.

Most weeks he worked five or six nights,

depending how the first five had gone. Some nights were slower than others, but he was starting to get himself regular customers who actually asked for him by name. One of these regulars was Jason Lee, a club owner in the city centre who Mark found himself running home most nights he worked and building up a bit of a friendship with.

Jason Lee had a fierce reputation and the first time Mark picked him up he recognised him straightaway. He lived on the outskirts of town in a huge house which given it was called 'The Lodge' bore no resemblance to any lodge Mark had ever seen. It had massive electric gates which Jason operated by remote control and then there was a long driveway up to a detached house sporting symmetrical turrets on either side; it was huge and Mark was very impressed. By all accounts Jason Lee was a local boy who had done good; he had a club in the city centre, but his fingers were certainly in lots of other pies and from what he had heard, not all of them were legal.

Mark liked him though, they would chat away through the whole journey and at the end there was always a generous tip. Jason had lost his driving licence, making the same journey that Mark took him on; one night the police had randomly stopped him at four in the morning and subsequently breathalysed him. A 12-month ban followed and Jason would often rant about how someone had set him up; somehow Mark thought that somewhere along the line Jason would find out who that someone was and then woe betide the person who had done it; Jason Lee wasn't the type of man he would like to cross.

But they were easy in each other's company. Jason

showed an interest in how the taxi was doing, or how Anna was, was Mark earning plenty on the taxi? If he wasn't Jason said there was always other ways to make an extra pound or two if Mark knew what he meant. He didn't really. He wasn't particularly streetwise; his youth had been spent playing football; training, matches; football had been his life. When it became apparent that he wasn't going to make it as a footballer he had secured an apprenticeship with a local firm. He might have been working with a load of Jack the lads, but Mark had kept himself to himself, happy to be able to afford a season ticket for his local team and glad he had money in his pocket for the odd night out with his mates. The whole drug culture had passed over his head; it just wasn't his scene.

So guessing that that was what Jason Lee was talking about, he said nothing. He didn't want anything to do with his shady business dealings. He would manage without going down that avenue; but he wouldn't. Anna left work and suddenly their money wasn't even stretching through the month. They just about had everything they needed for the baby, but they still struggled. They took out a couple of payday loans; the second was to pay the first and then they renewed the first to pay the second and so it went on. Each time the loans cost them more and more; it was a false economy; they might have paid the red letter bills that were outstanding, but the loans were crippling them.

A crisis somewhere in the Middle East pushed up fuel prices and Mark found that even working six nights a week, he wasn't taking home two thirds of what he had been doing a few months earlier. It was a worrying time and he found that he couldn't rest easy in his bed, something had to give. He looked around for other jobs where he would get a regular weekly income, but there was nothing, well, nothing that would pay as much as the taxi did, even in its fragile state. He tried to get a loan from the bank; that way he could pay off the payday loans, have a little bit of cash in the bank and have one single manageable loan payment to make every month. But the bank laughed him out of the branch. The erratic behaviour of his credit report put paid to any hope of a loan; there didn't seem to be any light at the end of the tunnel for him.

Anna was getting near her due date; he liked her, they got on well enough and even though he never envisaged settling down so early with her, they were okay. Aside from their money worries the future seemed to be bright for them. When her pains started he was with her all of the way. He held her hand and mopped her brow and when she pushed their beautiful daughter into the world he was there to see it all. Looking at his daughter wrapped in a pink blanket and placed in her mother's arms, he was so overcome with emotion he had to leave the room and go to the toilet. He hadn't expected to feel like that. He would die for those two girls in that room. His brand new daughter and the woman who gave him her. Even if they split up Anna would have a small part of his heart for what she had done for him.

And suddenly the goal posts were moved and he knew that he would do everything he could to make sure Anna and the baby had everything they needed. If that meant doing some work for Jason Lee, then so be it. Needs must and he needed money; more of it and more regularly. By the time Anna arrived home with baby India, he was on Jason Lee's payroll.

Jason taught him the ins and outs, a sort of apprenticeship in drug dealing. He knew the street names for each of the products and he knew the prices he could sell them for and the price Jason wanted in return. There was a good mark-up and there was money to be made; within days he had upped his income by at least £50 a day. He wasn't happy doing it; it made him nervous and he was forever waiting for the police to pull him over. He wasn't stupid though and only carried enough so that if he was pulled, there was not a lot more than there would be for his own personal use. The rest he kept hidden away. His mobile rang and bleeped constantly; shockingly so. He had no idea that there was such a demand. Jason initially put him out there but he started to generate his own customers too; there was no particular type, but he was starting to be able to spot potential buyers. Like Cha Cha. He felt bad about her; he had only wanted to help; he even sold the little pills to her cheaper than he did others; and he had warned her, he told her not to start using them regularly, but she had and now she was handing over to him a small fortune every week.

He thought of not selling her them, but knew she would soon find someone else who would be willing, they would charge her more and if he was honest he liked to keep an eye on her. She was turning into an addict before his very eyes and he felt like shit. She had her whole future ahead of her and she was putting it all in jeopardy. He wanted to help but didn't know how;

not without getting involved and then what?

The taxi radio crackled; he had a fare from one part of town to another. It was a ruse; he knew by the address where he was picking up that it was someone wanting more than a taxi ride. But it worked well; the customer would get in taxi, Mark would drive off and they would do their deal while they moved. At the end of the journey the customer would hand over the money and the goods would be handed back as if it was change; you just never knew who was watching. And that's how it was done every night.

His 'extra' customers came in all shapes and forms. Most he would have expected to dapple in drugs but there were others who shook him; a doctor, a solicitor, nurses, teachers; it seemed that there were no boundaries to the people who would contact him and hand the money over for a little something. He had even done dealing with a couple of pensioners; he couldn't imagine his own nana and granddad sitting in their little living room sharing a 'smoke'! But it was money and at the end of the day that was what he was doing it for; to look after Anna and India. His payday loans were long gone and even tipping over a fair amount to Anna every week, he was building himself a nice little nest egg.

Business was brisk; both on the taxi and in his other dealings. The city centre had been packed all night and the last couple of hours before he knocked off for the night were spent going forwards and backwards between his home town and the city. When Jason texted with a time he wanted picking up, he decided that he would call it a night; he already had a wad of cash in his jacket pocket so it wouldn't harm to go home a couple of hours earlier than he would normally have done. With a bit of luck he might catch India's 4am feed and let Anna have a bit more sleep.

He had been ill prepared for the emotions that India had stirred in him. She was just so perfect. It was the reason for the dodgy dealings, he wanted everything for her. But it was a double-edged sword; he might be providing for India but he was preying on someone else's child and the thought of India being in the same position as Cha Cha made him shudder. He would kill anyone who did that to India. He vowed that he would always look out for India and would never let her get into a similar position, a tall order, but he could try and at least he would have the added advantage of knowing the signs.

Jason was as punctual as ever as Mark pulled up. Jumping into the front seat they chatted away about the derby game, how busy the club had been and how the taxi had gone that night. Mark told him that business had also been swift with his other business too and as they did every night, Jason made a note of what Mark would need to replenish his stock and how much it would cost him. He wouldn't pick his new stock up from Jason; there would be someone contact him at some point the following day and Mark would treat the transaction like a fare; just like he did for his selling. Jason wasn't stupid enough to have anything with him at home but he took the money and Mark often wondered how much money went through the gates of The Lodge.

For once, Jason asked him if he would like to go in for a nightcap. Taken aback, he thought about India and decided against it. Declining politely, Jason went on to say that he had a shipment of some new stuff coming in, if he was interested. Cheap to buy, lucrative to sell, the mark-up on it was astonishing; did he want to give them a go? Mark used the few minutes of counting out Jason's money to think about it. What did he know about drugs? What did these actually do? He was getting himself in far too deep! But the extra money would come in handy; Anna had been talking about having India baptised and that wouldn't be cheap! *In for a penny; in for a pound!* he thought to himself, handing over the cash for Jason's stock and an extra £50 for the new supply. If he didn't do it someone else would and he couldn't really turn the extra cash down.

Jason took the bundle of cash off him; including £10, HE75 229564, which Cha Cha had handed to him earlier in the night. Deal done, Jason got out of the taxi and Mark turned it around and headed back down the drive and through the gates. He had barely got through when the gates closed behind him.

Later, at home feeding India, he couldn't shake off Cha Cha and the new pills he had ordered. Surely there was more to life than money! If he got caught it would be jail time for him and then what would happen to Anna and India? Finishing the feed, he placed India over his shoulder to wind her. He could feel her breathing on his neck and no matter how much he thought what he was doing was for her, he couldn't hold the tears back; he was in something he would struggle to get out of; he was in a much bigger mess!

10

The Best That Money Can Buy

He stood watching the rear lights of the taxi go down the drive and through the gates. Flicking the remote control, the gates swung closed and the grounds were secure again. He loved having the big remote house, but sometimes he wished they still lived in their little flat in the centre of town; it just felt so much safer. Jason hated the darkness and looking out towards the front gates, that's all he could see and he didn't like it.

But The Lodge was fitting for his status; Amanda loved it and had been there every step of the way when it was built. He had got the land from 'a friend' who owed him a bit of cash and as soon as he had showed it to his wife she had wanted to build the house of their dreams on it and had gone on and on at it until he agreed. But he would have preferred just to stay in the flat; it was handy for the town centre and only a 10-minute drive to the club. If the truth be known he blamed The Lodge for losing his driving licence; he always seemed to need a little drink before he got home; maybe he had started to have one or two too many. Anyway the licence was gone for another few months, but he thought that even when he was allowed to drive again he would stick to the taxi. He couldn't imagine coming home to the mausoleum of a home without a couple of drinks under his belt.

He didn't get it. He wasn't particularly frightened of anything; he owned a city-centre club and carried out dodgy deals every day; he had a reputation as a hard man, but this house put the willies up him, inside and out! He would do anything to move away from it but Amanda was having none of it; she liked nothing better than entertaining her family and friends there; especially around the indoor swimming pool. There was no way she would give it all up.

So he shut up and put up and tried not to react to the shivers. He meant to check out what the land had been used for before he was gifted it but always talked himself out of it. No one else seemed bothered by it, just him. Even Livvy, his 17-year-old daughter from his first marriage didn't seem to mind staying there; in fact if anything she loved being there, especially when she had some of her friends with her and they partied around the pool.

Making his way to the room he used as his home office and Amanda called his study, he made sure the front door was locked and the outside alarms activated. It wasn't just the things that he couldn't see that irked him; in his line of work there was always a threat from burglars and kidnappers. It was no wonder he never rested easy. He liked his office though; switching on the plasma TV screen, Sky News played out in the background while he sorted out his business before he went to bed.

Pouring himself a Jack Daniels, he sat at his desk and glanced at the headlines circulating along the bottom of the TV screen; happy there was nothing too interesting happening in the world, he counted up the cash and made a note of what he needed to do the following day. He hated having cash in the house but there was no way that he would leave it at the club and because he ran both businesses side by side, he needed to deal with it somewhere where he could concentrate; one false move and the tax man would be on him like a ton of bricks.

So there was one set of books for the club, where all the till receipts tallied with the money and everything was banked in a timely fashion to pay suppliers, staff and to give himself generous drawings that fit his lifestyle. And then there was another set that he kept for himself for the other business. These were kept as meticulously as the clubs were; he needed to know exactly what was happening at all times. He kept a kind of register listing all his 'boys and girls', what was selling well and making money and what wasn't. If any of his staff dropped in supply, he wanted to know why. It was an ever growing list on his register, times were hard and with it supply seemed to go up.

But Jason had his buttons sewn on and liked to think as 'drug barons' went, he was fair and approachable. Not that he thought himself as a 'drug baron'. He was a businessman and a bloody good businessman at that. The proof was in the pudding; he wouldn't be where he was if he wasn't; there was always someone knocking on his door, so to speak, someone who thought he was bigger and better. But Jason was smart and if they thought he could be bullied out of business they had knocked on the wrong door. In a different place with different opportunities he could have been like Sir Alan Sugar or Sir Richard Branson, but that would never happen. The only time he would have any dealings with Her Majesty would be if everything went tits up and he ended up doing time at Her Majesty's pleasure.

He couldn't grumble though; what did a title mean? He had everything he wanted. He had the best that money could buy. If he thought about what he had and where he had come from, he could barely recognise himself as the snotty kid in hand-me-down clothes with never a penny to his name. The youngest of seven, there was never enough of anything; food, money, clothes. What his brother wore to school one week he would wear the next just so people didn't realise that they barely had an outfit between them. They were hard times, not helped by the fact that anything they did have his dad would piss up the wall. His poor mam! It was no wonder she was so proud of him when he had opened his club and bought the flat in town. She was dead long before The Lodge was built, but he liked to think that she would see it from whichever star it was she was sitting on; he liked the thought of her watching him; keeping him safe just like she always had.

Jason's dad was in a care home in town; 91 years old now. Jason hardly saw him. He had been such an old bastard to them all that Jason found it hard to forgive him; even if he was a little old man now. He hadn't always been like that; he had been bigger than

Jason and thought nothing of knocking his kids and his mam around. Jason had a long memory and could especially remember his mam's screams as if they were yesterday; his mam would still be around today if she hadn't had so many beatings.

He gulped the Jack Daniels down and poured another. Taking the bundles of cash, he placed them into the safe; he would take the club's to the bank in the morning and he had a shipment coming in the day after tomorrow, so he would leave the rest in the safe until that was paid for. There was another small bundle on the desk; Amanda's. Every week he would give her a handful of money to get what she wanted through the week; she had a credit card as well and had never been shy about spending any of it. She was high maintenance and he paid the price for it. But he loved her; he must, he had left his first wife Paula and his only child Livvy for her. Painful memories.

He had fallen for Amanda the minute he had seen her. She had walked into his club and he knew without a shadow of a doubt that he had to have her. She wouldn't be his first indiscretion; it went with the territory, but Amanda had resisted his charms and his power and flatly refused to be a bit on the side. The more she wriggled away, the more he chased her until it got to such a point that Amanda was all he could think about; she consumed his every being.

Paula knew that there was something different going on. For years she had turned a blind eye to his latest young girl, but this time there was something different. Jason was wrapped around Amanda's little finger and he hadn't even kissed her; she was like Scotch mist – as soon as he thought he was getting somewhere with her she would be gone. At home he was like a bear with a sore head and both Paula and a three-year-old Livvy's lives weren't worth living. It wasn't even Amanda's fault, she didn't encourage him, he was a married man and as far as she was concerned he was a no-no! It didn't stop him though, he would turn up at her work to give her a lift home, he would take her for meals and days out, but there was absolutely nothing between them, they never even touched.

All the other girls that circled his waters faded into the background; against Amanda they were young and silly and even though he had found them attractive in the beginning and thought nothing of taking one or two of them to his bed either singly or together, now they held no interest and unfortunately neither did long-suffering Paula. Amanda was it; everything about her screamed out to him; her face; her hair; her body; her intellect and most of all her morals. She was no one's bit on the side and she had no intention of being Jason Lee's no matter how much of a Mr Big he was.

So he found himself packing his bags and leaving both Paula and Livvy; at the time he had no remorse about doing something so heartless, he had one mission and one mission alone. Amanda! Paula was furious; they had been together since they were kids; she had been with him when he had nothing and had helped him build up his empire, the legit side of it anyway. She had helped him beg, borrow and steal the money for the club and had scrubbed and painted the grubby old bingo hall until it twinkled with disco lights and became the in place to be in the city centre. He owed her and she knew he did. But if he was a shit as a husband and father, he had principals and without a second thought bought a brand new house for Paula and Livvy around the corner from her mam's.

Paula moved out of the flat and Jason moved back in. There was nothing stopping him being with Amanda now and satisfied that he was only a married man on paper now, Amanda succumbed and Jason's dreams came true. She was everything he knew she would be and how he loved her! He worshiped her body and he adored her mind. For her 21st birthday he bought her an MG sports car and the driving lessons to go with it. Money was no object and now that they were official she accepted every gift with excitement and rewarded him with her love. He was a happy man.

Where Paula was adamant that she wouldn't allow him to have anything to do with Livvy, it all changed when she met someone new of her own. Suddenly he wasn't an ogre and Amanda wasn't a trollop and Livvy started coming back to the flat to stay. Amanda loved the little girl and would take care of her when Jason went to work; she had already said that she didn't want children, but she loved spending time with the little girl and some weekends Jason would feel very left out when the 'girls' went off to the pictures or on a shopping trip.

When his divorce came through he took Amanda and her family, Livvy and a couple of close friends to Cyprus and they were married. She was 22 years old and he was 45. If he was expecting a trophy wife he was very much mistaken; she took an interest in the club, her advice priceless when it came to updating, revamping and getting bodies through the door. She came up with ideas to run promotions on quieter nights and helped employ staff that would be pleasing on the customers' eyes. She had packed her job in as soon as she and Jason had got together, so apart from helping out in the club now and again, mainly she had her days to herself. Aerobics, hairdressers, beauty salons, golf; her list of things she did was endless.

But she was loving and attentive with Jason; she cooked and even though she employed a cleaner for the flat, she kept it homely. Those first few years were the happiest in Jason's life. And then he got the plot of land and his loving wife turned into the project manager from hell; everything had to be just so and he would often feel sorry for the builders who had to dance to her tune. With regret – his, not hers – they packed up the flat and made the journey across town to their new house, a house that would never feel like home to him but where Amanda said all of her dreams had come true.

And so they settled. They threw lavish parties for their friends and Livvy all but moved in. The club thrived; every week it did just as well as the one before which was surprising in the recent climate, and his other business was doing well too. He had recently had a couple of hiccups; there seemed to have been police keeping an eye on one or two of his suppliers and they had been arrested. But there was nothing to lead them back to Jason and as quickly as one supplier fell another would stand on the fallen one and take his place. It was a young man's business though and he wondered how much longer he could keep up the ducking and diving; the people on his register were ever evolving and he knew that one lapse of judgement would bring the whole lot tumbling down.

Of course Amanda knew nothing of the second business. She assumed all of the money came from the club and he wanted to keep it that way. If the worst happened at least she could honestly say that she knew nothing about it and he might be able to keep her out of trouble. He had enough money stashed away for both Amanda and Livvy to get away if they needed to and his solicitor knew what to do if it happened. But for now he would keep going. Maybe he would retire altogether in a few years' time, sell the lot and spend half the year living in the Costa del Crime; Amanda would love that, she liked nothing better than to holiday in Marbella. He was sure she wouldn't mind putting down roots there for a while, if he could get her away from The Lodge, that was.

He switched off the TV and locked up the office. Making his way up the marble staircase he did one of his shudders; it really was a creepy place. The light was on in the bedroom, but Amanda was sleeping soundly. She had hated him working nights when they had first got together, but she was used to them now. She looked so young lying there in the bed, his heart constricted just like it had the first time he had seen her. She was in her 30s now, but looked younger. She made him laugh talking about having a facelift when the time came, but that was a long way off, there wasn't a line on her face. The only bit of work she had done was have a boob job. Jason didn't think she needed it, but what Amanda wanted was what Amanda got and even though he was loath to admit it, they were magnificent!

Opening her bedside drawer he put her money in.

There was £200 in a picture of £20 and £10 notes, HE75 229564 included. *That should see the week out for her,* he thought to himself. And she always had her credit card to use if there wasn't enough. He didn't want her going short.

He had himself a quick shower and slid into bed next to Amanda. He didn't like the dark, never had done from being little, so he left the bedside lights on. He lay staring at the ceiling for a long time, his mind jumping from one thing to the next until eventually he could feel his eyelids begin to drop. Almost asleep, a shudder ran through his body. *This bloody house...* he thought to himself before sleep took over and he was gone.

11

A Gold Digger

Amanda Lee woke up the minute her husband Jason got into bed. She lay pretending she was asleep while he lay beside her sighing and waiting for sleep to come. She thought about telling him she was awake, but then thought better of it and feigned sleep until he was snoring soundly and she could get up without disturbing him.

Throwing on her dressing gown and fishing out her slippers from under the bed, she made her way downstairs. She loved being up first thing in the morning. Making herself a cup of coffee she made her way into the conservatory where she opened the blinds and sat in one of the chairs placed in the window. It was getting light and because the conservatory was long and narrow and ran out into the lawn, she felt like she was sitting in the middle of the garden. She loved it. She curled up in the chair and sipped on her coffee. She had fell on her feet the day she had met Jason Lee.

She knew of him, of course, before she met him. One of her friends had been one of his 'girls' so she knew how he ticked. He was a married man and got away with what he could when he could. Before she had even met him she was determined she wasn't going to be one of the many, she was going to be the 'one'! It helped that he was good looking; very good looking for a man his age; all she had to do was stick to her plan and he would be putty in her hands.

Amanda Johns was 19 when she met Jason. She most certainly set her cap at him, but even though he chased and begged and pleaded with her to sleep with him, she stuck to her guns and refused point blank. He was married and there was no way she was going to be just a bit on the side. So she kept to her game plan and let him take her out for drinks and meals and all the time she kept to her 'you can look but you can't touch!' And it worked!

Jason had no idea that he had been played. He thought that she had just stumbled into his club one night by chance. But she didn't, she had it all planned out. Julia, her friend, had told her all about him and she had seen him driving around town in his flash cars. She hated her life. She had left school thinking she would walk straight into a modelling job and at first it had seemed possible. But the whole business was filled with dirty old and young men and it seemed that to get anywhere she had to give more than photographs of her body away. She walked away from it and took the first job she could get; receptionist at an opticians. It was the most boring way to spend her days ever and the pittance she was paid at the end of the month did nothing to encourage her. When Julia told her about Jason Lee, the money, the girls, she started to think that maybe he could be a meal ticket out of the monotony. But she wanted it all. She was better than Julia and the other girls, she wasn't going to just be a flash in the pan. He obviously wasn't happy at home or else he wouldn't have wandered in the first place, so surely it wouldn't be too hard to take him away from there. Even though she knew there was a kid involved she didn't see it as a problem, not if she eventually befriended her, because she had no intention of having any kids of her own. No, Jason's little girl was very much part of the plan too.

So the night she happened to chance into the club with a couple of mates, she made sure she was looking a million dollars. And she made sure that he not only saw her, but he saw her chatting to Julia, one of his barmaids. It worked and before the night was even out he had asked for her number. The rest was easy. At first he lusted after her, then when he got to know her a bit better he fell in love with her. By keeping him out of her bedroom, he became obsessed and the more obsessed he was the more she saw him, until eventually he packed up and left his wife.

By the time he had bought his estranged wife a house and he moved back into the flat, she was at his side. When little Livvy started coming to stay everything was in place. Livvy was so easy to love and they bonded easily and were still close even though she was now a spoilt stroppy teenager. The wedding quickly followed the divorce and she was the happiest girl in the world. Even though she had set out to get him, she really liked him, loved him even. He was kind and generous and he was interested in what she had to say. He didn't mind that she packed her receptionist's job in and spent her days doing virtually nothing and he took on board what advice she gave him about the club. She didn't even mind helping in the club, she liked it, it was like a night out and she was good with people. Whereas the bar staff probably wouldn't say anything to Jason about any grievances they had, they didn't mind telling Amanda and she would act as a kind of mediator. The same with customers, she listened to what they liked or didn't like about the club and did what she could to put things right.

When Jason mysteriously acquired a plot of land she really wasn't as green as she thought she was; she nagged and nagged at him until he took her across to see it. It was a huge piece of uncared for wasteland, but to her it was paradise. She could see a house with lawns and a long winding driveway. This was her dream. Jason couldn't see it and said he just wanted to sell the land on, but she was having none of it and drew little pictures of the house so he could see what she saw. And like everything else she wanted, she got it. For 18 months she travelled across town every day to supervise the builders. She was a bitch, she knew she was, but it was her way or the highway and the builders soon got wind of that and didn't so much as build a wall without Amanda being there.

She knew they resented her; she was loads younger than most of them on site. She had heard them when they were on their cigarette or tea breaks: 'She's a gold digger, he's old enough to be her father!' She didn't care, it was her house they were building, where were they going home to on a night? Nothing like the home she would have so they could bitch all they liked. And they were right, Jason was older than her dad, and her mam, it wasn't about age. She had watched her mam and dad struggle to bring her and her younger brothers up, they hadn't had a youth of their own. Her mam had got pregnant before she had left school, so they had gone from school to parenthood in one stride. After Amanda there had been three more babies and that had been one of the very reasons she didn't want kids of her own. She had been brought up by kids with kids and she had had enough!

Shocked as they were that she had got it together with Jason Lee, they couldn't really say anything when they saw her lifestyle and they were always keen to accept any bits of cash or presents she gave. When Amanda had suggested that they kept the flat they were leaving as an investment for the future to Jason, he agreed and even more strangely agreed to her family moving in rent free to act as caretakers; he would do anything to keep his Amanda happy and so an ecstatic John's family moved into the luxury four-bedroom apartment that they had only ever seen in the pages of magazines. Having a sugar daddy for a husband certainly had its advantages.

The Lodge was amazing. It was everything she could have dreamed of and even though she knew Jason wasn't really happy there, she was, and if she was happy then she would go out of her way to make Jason happy too. It was huge – six bedrooms, two living rooms, a kitchen that ran the length of the rear of the house. A gym, indoor swimming pool and sauna and the conservatory she was sitting in. It was something else and although it was worth well over a million, it had cost a fraction of that to build, thanks to her canny project managing and purchases. Money hadn't been an object, mind, Jason had given her an open purse, but even he was flabbergasted when she showed him her spreadsheets to what the build had actually come in at and the value the estate agent had put on it. And that was before the gardens had been done, they were something else all on their own and she delighted in them every day.

The Lodge had been her choice of name too. She had gone to the local library and checked the archives for the land's history. Once upon a time there had been a lodge on the perimeter of their land belonging to some lord or other who lived in the main house about five miles away. What she also found out was that the family that lived in the lodge had been burnt to death, though there were no records saying that it had been done deliberately or if it had been an accident. All the newspaper article had said was that the man and the woman had been employees of the lord and their bodies had been found in the burnt-out building. Of course she didn't mention this information to Jason; he was freaked out enough about the place, but Amanda had never felt frightened. Quite the opposite really, she felt safer there than she had ever felt in her life.

Without the building work to oversee Amanda had to find other ways to fill her days. Jason was with her most mornings, but by lunchtime he would be off doing something and she would be left to her own devices for the rest of the day. She joined a gym, but soon lost interest because she could quite as easily use the gym at home, so she booked in to do some classes and quite enjoyed them. She did the usual girly things like hairdressers and beauty salons, but apart from her mam, she didn't really have anyone to do the stuff with. Her mam was always game for anything though and a new, better relationship developed between them. There were only 16 years between them and they were more like sisters instead of mother and daughter, especially after all the treats to the hairdressers her mam was party to.

Apart from that though, there was little else. The Lodge gardens still needed cultivating, but Amanda wasn't sure what could be done, so she rang the experts and Brian Harrison arrived in his little van, sketch pad in hand, and spent the next three days designing what Amanda thought would be the most beautiful gardens in the area. It would take time and money, but as always Jason was generous with the money and Amanda became generous with her time.

Even when Brian wasn't there, she would spend hours and hours digging borders, planting shrubs and watering the newly laid lawns. Brian showed her how to take care of each thing that went into the garden and he even tolerated her ever changing demands. Six months later the gardens were unrecognisable; they were her pride and joy and something she showed off to anyone who had time to come and see them.

There was a pond with koi fish, and a small area at the side that could be used as a golf driving range if Jason ever dusted off the golf clubs he kept in the garage. There were lawns and rockeries and in the spring the lawns were covered in snowdrops, crocuses and daffodils. It was Amanda's piece of paradise and when there was nothing else to do, she would tend the garden as best she could. If the weather was bad she would sit in the conservatory and watch out of the windows, just like she was doing that morning as the new day dawned.

She was often up at that hour; usually she would have gone to bed early with a book and fallen asleep before she had even finished the first page, but then Jason would disturb her when he came to bed in the early morning hours. Sometimes she would let him know she was awake and they would chat or whatever else took their fancy. But lately she had been pretending she was asleep. She was in trouble and she didn't know what she was going to do.

Drew Harrison, Brian the gardener's son, had come bounding into her life three months earlier. Surprised to find out that Brian even had a son, more surprised that he was the most handsome man she had ever seen in her life and even more surprised that she had fallen for him.

Amanda had come back from one of her classes one morning to find Brian in the garden showing a young man around. Not fazed, Brian had had a key fob for the gates since he had started work, she pulled up in her car and gave him a cheery wave. Showered and coffee in hand, she made her way out into the garden to ask Brian about one of the fish being a bit wobbly. Brian proudly introduced her to his son, Drew, who he said was training to be a police officer. She smiled up at him, trying not to show how uncomfortable she was having a policeman on her property, but that was to be the least of her problems. The face that smiled down at her was the most perfect specimen of a man that she had ever seen in the flesh.

She didn't even think that he was a man yet, he was still a boy, but he made her go weak at the knees just looking at him. Never one to be fazed by anything, she quickly pulled herself together and ushered them over to the pond where one of the little goldfish was lolling about in the corner. On safer ground again, they chatted about the fish and Amanda walked away as Brian fished it out and put the little thing out of its misery.

And that should have been the end of her contact with Drew Harrison, but of course it wasn't. Funny thing was she didn't mention Drew, the would-be policeman, being at the house to Jason. The less he knew about his existence the better, some inner voice told her. For one, she knew that Jason would find a reason to get rid of Brian and for two, she wanted to keep Drew to herself. So she said nothing; after all, if Jason couldn't tell her about his business dealings, why would she think that there could be a problem with a copper being on the premises? But she knew all about Jason and how he made his money, she had known before she had even met him. She pretended she knew nothing because that was the way he liked it; she was his little woman and apart from the odd suggestion about the club here and there, he liked to keep her well out of the picture.

The following week when she went into the fitness centre for her yoga class, Drew Harrison was in the reception. She wasn't in the least bit surprised, she had somehow been expecting to bump into him somewhere. He was dressed in his gym clothes and looked like he had been for a workout. She hadn't seen him there before and she knew if she had, she would remember him. There was no way she could ignore him; she didn't want to, so she walked over and asked him if he wanted to go and get a coffee. Skipping class, it was the start of something she was powerless to get out of.

Amanda had never been with anyone just for the sake of it. Everyone she had ever been with had been a means to an end, the ultimate prize being Jason and everything he could give her. Drew Harrison had nothing. He wasn't even a trainee policeman anymore; he hadn't passed his medical which she found hard to believe, but what did she know? He said he was at a crossroads; his dad wanted him to go into the family business but he wasn't sure. He was so young; 21, Amanda was 33. As he sat chatting to her across the table in the little café along the road from the fitness centre, she had never wanted anyone so physically in all of her life.

It seemed that he felt the same. They had exchanged mobile numbers and from then on in she was a slave to it. She constantly checked it for messages which started off friendly and chatty and gradually became more and more intense. She had to be careful; she had never had a reason not to leave her mobile lying all over the house, now she constantly had it in her pocket or hid it away in her handbag. She felt like a giddy teenager, a feeling that had passed her by in her youth. Drew was attentive; when Jason had gone to work and she was free to text him back without fear of being caught, the texts flew backwards and forwards.

She wanted to see him, but didn't know where. Jason knew everyone everywhere but worse than that, people knew who she was even if she had never seen them before in her life. Drew came up with a solution; he started to work with his dad so one day a week he would arrive in his dad's little van and work in Amanda's vast gardens. Jason met him, he couldn't not; but the garden, like the house was his wife's domain and he didn't take a lot of notice of the blond Adonis that had arrived in the garden.

From then on it was snatched kisses whenever they could, careful not to arise Brian's suspicions or anyone else who came to carry out jobs in the house. And once he knew his way around and everyone was used to seeing him, he would come back on his own steam on the pretence of doing some work in the garden, in fact it wasn't a pretence; he would get the mower out of the shed and ride around the garden on it. But when there was no one about, Amanda took him to her bed. Together they were everything that she thought they would be, she couldn't keep her hands off his young taut skin and she couldn't get enough of him.

She felt like Lady Chatterley; it was a huge buzz. But it was also a very dangerous game. Jason would kill him and her if he ever got wind of what was going on right under his nose. For the first time in Amanda Lee's life she was in love; she was in lust and she was in trouble.

When Jason surprised her with a two-week holiday to Marbella she wanted to cry. With a huge smile on her face, her head was spinning around and around. What was she going to do without Drew for two weeks? Worse, what was she going to do with Jason? Because that was another upshot of her relationship with Drew; she didn't want Jason. Whereas it had never bothered her that he was twice her age, she had even found him attractive and had never had a problem with the intimate side of their relationship, now she had Drew and his toned body, Jason just didn't do it for her.

Drew assured her it would be fine, that he would be there waiting for her when she got back and she could text or ring him if she could safely do so. Off she went to Spain. It was a miserable holiday, not that Jason would have noticed; she painted a smile on her face and played the doting wife just as she always had. Whereas before it hadn't been a hardship, now it was purgatory and she knew that there was no way that she could live her life like that anymore. She needed to leave Jason and be with Drew, but even with her sharp mind and ability to connive and plot, she didn't have a clue how she was going to do it.

He was as good as his word and was there for her when she got back. They picked up where they left off; if she thought that the whole thing was just physical, just a fling, she would have just let it run its course. But her feelings ran deep and so did Drew's; he was taking a huge risk just being with her. Jason Lee had quite the reputation and although he wasn't the type of man who got his own hands dirty, he knew men who did things like that for fun. He loved her. Amanda wasn't a dizzy blonde, she was astute and knew how people ticked; who was real and who wasn't. Drew Harrison was real. But he was also fickle and that worried her.

Still living at home, now working for his dad, if she left Jason they wouldn't have a lot. She would be entitled to some kind of settlement; if they sold The Lodge alone there would be a sizeable amount of money so that they could get a place of their own and she could start again. But what of the future? Drew was no businessman, it would be her that would have to use all her skills to give them some kind of comfortable lifestyle; she wouldn't be poor again, not even for love. And then there was her family! Would Jason kick them out of the flat if she left? She was a victim of her own success. She had made Jason Lee fall in love with her, worship her, and now because of that she knew that he wouldn't let her go easily.

It was daylight before Amanda shook herself out of her ponderings; the coffee had gone cold and her back ached because she had sat so long. She needed to get a move on, she had a hairdresser's appointment in town at nine and parking at that time of day was horrendous. Jason was still flat out as she made her way through the bedroom to the shower and he remained that way while she dressed and took her 'housekeeping' money out of her bedside drawer. Generous to a fault as always.

She sat the two hours in the hairdressers whilst she had her colour redone and let the mindless chatter of the stylist go over her head. Usually it was a treat, but today it felt like purgatory; her mind danced from here to there and then back again. Drew texted; he wanted to meet her in town; did she have any cash on her? Could she lend him £50? That was one of the drawbacks; he was useless with money! Now used to having cash whenever she needed it, she would struggle having to start to watch the pennies again. But what could she do?

She paid the £120 for her hair on her credit card and counted out £50 to hand over to Drew. She had it, he needed it, what hardship was it for her? She could always ask for more; Jason never asked what she did with her money. He was standing near her car just like she had told him to be. The meeting had to look like a coincidence; she just never knew who might see them. So they chatted for a couple of minutes and as she made to fumble in her bag for her car keys, she dropped it along with the £50 that Drew retrieved along with her handbag. Rolled up in the bundle of notes was £10, HE75 229564. Waving him a cheery goodbye, he strode off down the street. Physically he never failed but to take her breath away.

But she had doubts – major doubts. She loved him and wanted him and wanted to be with him. But it was a huge ask of both of them; they would have to move away and then there was the money thing. She had worked so hard to get what she had! She didn't think she had much choice though. The gods had thrown her a joker and she didn't know what to do.

She was pregnant; at least two months by her reckoning. Amanda Lee, gangster's moll, savvy and streetwise, had got herself up the duff by the gardener. It would be laughable if it wasn't so tragic. Amanda hadn't wanted kids; she had Livvy and that was enough. So she had asked Jason to have the snip. What Amanda wanted Amanda got!

12

Take the Money and Run

He watched her walk out of the hairdressers, down the street and towards her car. Amanda Lee was a fine figure of a woman, stunning in fact, but as he made his way towards her he was nervous and he could tell she was too. The walls had eyes as well as ears and they never knew who would be watching them. So they played a game of 'fancy meeting you here' and chatted for a couple of minutes. Drew had asked her for some cash and as always she had given it to him, she had even done a bit of ad-libbing and dropped her handbag so he could pick the cash up without suspicion. It was a game. But it was a dangerous game and he was out of his depth.

It had started as a bit of fun; well, it had for him. His dad had told him all about Amanda Lee long before he had even been to The Lodge, and her dodgy husband Jason. Brian had said that she was years and years younger than Jason, but she knew her mind and despite reservations, Brian had enjoyed working on the grounds. So Drew had a fair idea about her before he had even had sight of her. Jason he knew more about; he had been a police cadet and people talked. He had quite a reputation in the area, both as a successful club owner and a notorious drug dealer; he was a bit of a Mr Big by all accounts and Drew was wary of his dad even working on the gardens for him.

Amanda had simply taken his breath away. She was nothing like he had imagined; he had expected to see some kind of Barbie doll, but she was far from it. Yes she was a blonde, but her hair was more a natural shade of blonde and it fell long and naturally down her back. She wasn't all fake tan and make-up; she didn't need it, she was a natural. The first morning he had seen her she had been to the gym and even though she had showered on her return, she was still just wearing a pair of jogging bottoms, tee-shirt and trainers. With her hair still damp from the shower she was a sight for sore eyes and as cock sure as he was in himself, he knew she had thought the same about him.

She was a challenge. From what his dad had told him they had a happy marriage. There was a daughter by his first marriage, but they had never had kids of their own. Instead they had their amazing house and holidayed whenever the urge took them. If they thought she was going to be arsey and full of herself, they were mistaken there too. She was quiet and interesting and interested in everything that was going on around her. If she was married to a ruthless gangster, it hadn't rubbed off on her and he was surprised that when his dad had to remove a dying fish from the pond, she had to walk away. Amanda Lee was an enigma to him and he wanted her.

And like Amanda Lee, what he wanted he got. At 21 he had had more women in his life than he could remember. When he was younger he used to put a notch in his headboard so to speak; he had realistically lost count years ago, but he knew there had been lots. Old, young; he wasn't really bothered, if she tickled his fancy then she was on his radar and he would eventually have her. Not one of them had stayed around long. As soon as they realised that they wouldn't be the only girl in his life, they would be off. He couldn't blame them. The grass was always greener on the other side for Drew Harrison.

He hadn't always been a looker. As a kid he had been quite the opposite; little, carrying a little bit too much weight and wearing glasses, no one took much notice of him. But then puberty kicked in and whereas his mates broke out in spots or grew upwards and resembled bean poles, Drew had grown overnight into a man. A very handsome man. Ditching the glasses and wearing contacts, his new look opened up a whole new world to 13-year-old Drew. The world of women.

Losing his virginity shortly after his 13th birthday, he would liken his life to a big box of Quality Street. He had to munch his way through every single chocolate in the box to determine what he liked and what he didn't like. He liked them all, every shape and every size. He was a pig, a glutton, and the more he had the more he wanted. No one was off limits, even at school it wasn't just his peers, he had even had a 'thing' with a teacher or two and even one of the dinner nannies, who wasn't a nanny at all, just a hot mamma.

Naturally bright, he did well at school despite all of the distractions, staying on to do his A Levels. His mam and dad were flabbergasted when he was accepted into university. It wasn't what he wanted though; the thought of sitting in a classroom for another three or four years was something that didn't appeal to him. Instead he thought about the fire brigade or the police force. Being a fireman appealed more, they had a certain type of reputation, it would be right up his street, but his eyesight wasn't good enough and he fell at the first hurdle.

So police force it was and he enrolled as a student officer, while he prepared to sit the entrance exam. The police uniform might not have had the same appeal as a fireman's, but it seemed girls like men in any type of uniform and even when he wasn't wearing it, the very mention of it made women fall at his feet. But of course it got him into trouble. He passed the entrance exam with flying colours, just like he knew he would, and then it was off to do some residential training. And that was where he became undone. Used to having who he wanted when he wanted, being caught in a compromising position with a fellow student officer soon put paid to any career in the police he had hoped for. He knew it wasn't allowed, but the little future WPC was just so cute. It was stupid and they were both out on their ears before their training had even finished.

Of course he didn't tell his mam and dad the real reason, he said he had failed his next medical, they assumed it was because of his eyesight and he didn't correct them. With limited options open to him his dad had asked him to work with him in the landscaping business. Never really interested before, he was interested in The Lodge and Amanda Lee. When his dad suggested he went to have a look around The Lodge with him to see what was his pride and joy, Drew went with him in the hope of seeing Amanda Lee and what all the fuss was about.

And of course he wasn't disappointed. He had Amanda on his radar and the following week found him standing in the reception at the leisure club she used for her yoga classes. It might have seemed like a moment of serendipity to her, but it was very much plotted by him. And she fell for it and for his charms as he led her away from the centre without her having a second thought for her class. That was the beginning; the chase was on. He had rarely had to chase after anyone; they usually fell at his feet and he would be bored with them before he had even got to know them.

This was different; it was a longer game. Texts, phones calls, snatched conversations and for the first time in a long time if not even his life, he found himself falling for her. She was funny and clever and she knew something about everything. She was no dumb blonde and she certainly wasn't a trophy wife; Drew had the feeling that Jason's club remained the place to be seen largely thanks to Amanda.

And then it happened; they tumbled into her bed and he was lost. It wasn't even the fact that she was older than him, he had had older, lots of them. It was her; it was the smell of her skin and the touch of her hands on his body. He fell hard and he knew that she felt the same. He knew for certain an affair was something that Amanda had never done before, but it was dangerous and they spent all of their time looking over their shoulders or listening for doors opening. Jason would kill him, he had no delusions about that. But he was in and there was no way out. She was an addiction and like all addictions, in the end they killed you if you didn't wean yourself off them.

A chance to go cold turkey came when Jason whisked Amanda away to Spain for a couple of weeks. He was pleased; he needed some thinking time and without her being on tap, he would have chance to think about what they were going to do and if they did do anything, what the consequences would be. He had nothing; less than nothing – he had debts. Amanda was used to having everything. He knew that she wouldn't walk away from the marriage with nothing, but with what she did have, how long would that last? There was no way she could live the lifestyle she had been accustomed to. It was all a bit of a mess.

She flew off and Drew sulked; he couldn't believe how much of his day was spent texting or talking or being with her. Within a few months of meeting her she had turned his life upside down. Without a shadow of a doubt he knew he loved her! But he wasn't happy; she said she would ring or text. She had been away five days and he had heard nothing. A new sensation took over his body. He was jealous. He had never been jealous of anything or anyone, apart from the obvious ones like David Beckham or Lewis Hamilton, but he had never been jealous of the thought of another man crawling over his girl's body. All of a sudden that was all he could think about. Jason pawing at Amanda; her in a little bikini, Jason untying it; the thoughts just went around and around.

It was eating him alive.

When his mates suggested a night out in the city he jumped at the chance. He needed distracting from the tormenting demons in his head and a drink-fuelled night out was just what was needed. He hadn't meant to go with anyone; he hadn't so much as looked at anyone since he met Amanda. But the drink kicked in and there were so many young girls out and about to choose from and of course old habits die hard and the inevitable happened.

She was young – very young – and pretty and she was probably as drunk as he was. Her mates mingled with his and when a party was suggested he followed along. The following morning he woke in a strange bed in a strange house with a strange girl by his side. He was mortified; Amanda hadn't even been gone a week and he was back to his old ways. The girl was all smiles even though she said she had the hangover from hell. In different circumstances he might have hung around a while with her. But he felt like shit and made excuses about going to work and left. He hadn't even asked her name.

And in his drunken stupor he had missed Amanda's call. The text she had sent was all about how much she missed and loved him and she would try and call again when she got the chance. He was the biggest shit in the world and vowed that it would never ever happen again and until Amanda arrived back home, all tanned and gorgeous, he thought of no one but her.

They picked up where they had left off. He told her he loved her and he meant it and she said the same and he was certain she meant it too. They talked about the future. He had nothing to offer her; he told her he understood if she decided that she wanted to stay. But she said she didn't want Jason anymore, she would live on nothing if she had to. He didn't quite believe her but the promise of it was nice!

Working in the gardens one morning, he was paying particular attention to some stubborn weeds on the decking area when he saw her. She hadn't seen him; she was in the pool area of the house and was fiddling with one of the loungers and all her concentration was on that. A shudder ran through his body and confusion filled his head. What the hell was SHE doing there? He would have recognised her anywhere; the titian-coloured hair was a complete giveaway, but he never forgot a face, it was a lesson he had learned long ago. He never ever forgot a face he had slept with even if he didn't know her name. But he knew her name. As he continued to stare at her, she must have realised and looked up at him. Any doubts he may have had were gone. It was the girl from the party weeks earlier.

The blood drained out of his body. The only person that she could be was Livvy Lee. What had he done? She smiled and waved and picking up a gown, she made for the door and slid it open. 'Hi, I didn't know you worked here!' He wanted to run, but stood rooted to the spot while she asked him questions and he politely asked her some in return. No doubt about it; this was Livvy Lee, Jason's daughter. Of all of the girls in the whole of the city he had picked Amanda's stepdaughter. If Amanda found out it would be curtains for him and he couldn't bear the thought of that. He had to think on his feet and before he really had chance to think the situation through, he had asked Livvy for her mobile number.

What he didn't want her to do was go blabbing in the house, so he said as nonchalantly as he could, 'Don't say anything; I can't see your mam and dad been happy you knocking about with the gardener!' She smiled at him; she really was a pretty little thing, he thought to himself.

'Of course I won't!' she said, laughing and returning into the house.

He hadn't even been gone five minutes when he sent her a text. 'Drink tonight?' And so it began. The double life. Amanda and Livvy. Stepmother and stepdaughter; with one common denominator – Jason Lee. His life was over and it was nobody's fault but his own. He spent time with Amanda when he could, but he spent more time with Livvy; and the more time he spent with Livvy, the more he liked her. She didn't have the certain something that Amanda had, but she was funny and clever and generous and even though she came from money and had been educated privately, she had nothing about her. The two females in his life were as different as chalk and cheese; but somehow they had both got through to him in different way.

It couldn't last though; one or both of them would find out about each other, then what? He would have nothing. As fate would have it, it came to a head much, much quicker than he would ever have imagined. Livvy was pregnant; they had been careful, well, apart from the first time when neither of them could really remember anything. She had bought a test and it had come back positive and so did the next and the next. She wanted to keep it; tell her mam and dad and Amanda, then the cat would be truly out of the bag. Panic was starting to paralyse him; he was done for. Yes, her mam and dad would probably be fine about it eventually, he didn't have to be a gardener forever; he was intelligent and if circumstances had been different Jason might have found him a little job in his business.

But in reality that was never going to happen. Amanda would never allow it; she was risking everything for him and he had thrown it all back in her face. Something his mam always said to him reverberated around his head. 'There's no revenge like a woman scorned!' And he knew hand on heart that Amanda would destroy him; and Livvy, she was an innocent in all this mess and she didn't deserve to be hurt. Neither did Amanda; he loved her.

So he was going to do the only thing that he could. He was running and leaving the mess behind him. If he stayed he had the feeling that he would be wearing a pair of concrete boots and ending up at the bottom of the River Tyne. Drew was a coward. It was a mess of his own making, but there was no way out without one or two or all of them being hurt. He had a friend in London; he had already made the telephone call. He had asked Livvy to hold off telling her parents until she was at least three months, and loving, trusting Livvy agreed. What he had really meant was, 'Don't tell them until I've gone!' He had borrowed bits of money from each of them over the previous couple of weeks; he had sold one or two belongings and today was the day he was going. The last bit of money from Amanda was the last he would need. She hadn't even asked why he had wanted it; *Easy come, easy go,* he had thought. Same with Livvy, he asked and she gave.

Well, he had taken the money and now he was going to run. He felt like a complete bastard as he walked away from Amanda. He resisted the temptation of turning around to look at her one last time; he didn't want her to be suspicious. Maybe she would be tomorrow or the next day when he hadn't texted or she hadn't been able to get through to him. Just like Livvy, he had sort of told her he was going to be busy the next week and gullibly she had believed him.

By then he would be long gone. But unexpectedly his heart was breaking. The mess he had woven would mean that after he had gone, he wouldn't be able to see his mam and dad, not for a while anyway, but he would make sure that they knew he was safe and well. He was on his way to sell his mobile; he took the SIM card out and threw it into a bin he passed. Mobile sold, he would have to use an old one he had fished out of his bedside drawer earlier in the day; one no one knew the number of.

An hour later he was walking into the Central Station with his rucksack on his back. He couldn't think about what he was doing, all he knew was that he had to go and he had to go now. He went to the ticket booth and booked a one-way ticket on the next train to London's King's Cross; from there he would make his way across London to his friend's flat in Blackheath. Then he would begin again, 300 miles away from Amanda and Livvy. He didn't know if Livvy would go ahead with the baby; he had a feeling she would. It was going to take all of his resolve not to come home, not for a long time anyway.

The lady behind the ticket office glass took his money, handed him his change and printed off his ticket. It had cost over £100. One of the notes he handed over was HE75 229564. The ticket seller separated the £10 notes from the £20 notes and put them into her till.

Now he had only to make his way to his platform and wait for his train. The urge to turn around and go home was strong. It took Drew everything he had to conjure Jason Lee's face. That was all it took for him to break into a run. He had taken Jason Lee's girls; he had taken their money and now he was running as if his life depended on it. It probably did!

13

Creative Accounting!

orna Smith stood in the queue at the Central Station ticket office. As she stood shuffling forward, she was kicking herself; she had been supposed to buy these tickets weeks ago; she had had the money but it had never made it into her bank account and now all the special offer tickets were gone. She was an idiot; her bad management was costing her £70! Well strictly she wasn't an idiot; it was just one of those things and she should have told her friends when they arranged the trip that she didn't actually have a bank account of her own!

By the time she got to the front of the queue she had counted and recounted the money about ten times. The tickets were £30 each, she needed seven so that was £210; she had £220 in her hand. Handing over the money, she waited for the ticket lady to print off the tickets and hand her her change. Stuffing the tickets and change, £10 – HE75 229564, into her handbag, she made her way out of the station and started on her journey home.

She was turning 40 that weekend; the trip to York

had been her friends' idea and she was looking forward to it. They were getting an early train, doing a bit of shopping, lunch, then drinks and back on the train at 10pm. She hadn't planned to do anything; she wasn't one for birthdays, but her friends were adamant and she sort of got swept along in the excitement. She just hoped that she didn't have to wear a banner and a badge, she didn't like being the centre of attention.

Another queue at the bus stop and a packed bus; she hadn't thought about rush hour when she had made her way into the city centre earlier in the afternoon. The bus in had been almost empty and the couple of shops she had popped into hadn't seemed too bad; apart from Primark which always seemed to be chocker-block no matter when you went in. But she had forgotten that come 5pm the offices would empty and the city would start to exit via the buses and hundreds of cars that were bumper to bumper on all of the roads.

She had never worked in the city; hardly even been in recently. For the past few years she just worked from home and she liked it that way. How did people do this every day? Surely it added loads of time onto their working day! But city-centre salaries were bigger and there were far more opportunities. She lived on the outskirts of a town and had learned the hard way that there was a limited amount of jobs available; but then she had gone for jobs with bad press; not hers, but the mud had stuck to her and no one had wanted to employ her.

That was a long time ago though; a different life in a different time. If she spoke to anyone about that time she would say that it happened in her previous life and people would laugh. She could even smile about it now, but it hadn't always been like that. She had lost everything and the repercussions were still reverberating through her life all these years later. But for the minute she was fine; she liked what she did for a living; she had good friends and at that minute she thanked God that she didn't work in the city centre.

She had been on the bus almost half an hour. Usually she would be home in that time, the bus had hardly made any headway; it just started and stopped and Lorna had to keep wiping the condensation off the windows so she could see out. It was dark and apart from the headlights of other vehicles there was nothing to look at. But it was better than having to strike up conversations with fellow passengers. If she had known she was going to be on the bus so long she would have brought her book. She could see it now sitting on her bedside table waiting for her to settle herself down for the night and carry on where she had left off the night before. For the life of her she couldn't remember what it was about. She could see its cover, but the story was lost. That was the thing about being an avid reader; one book bled into another and sometimes she actually lost the plot.

She leant her head against the window, ignoring the fact that her hair would be wet from the condensation running down it, and closed her eyes. She wasn't tired; just weary. The noise on the bus had started to set her nerves on edge; she wasn't used to crowds of people and she could feel the familiar throb of a headache starting. The woman sitting next to her was talking on her mobile phone; mindless chatter about where she had been at the weekend and with whom. Did the whole bus really want to know all that? Another girl in front of her was listening to music through her earphones; in-between her other companion's drawl, she could hear the songs. 'Broken Strings'! She would know that song anywhere; many a night she had cried herself listening to it on her CD.

The headache intensified and there was the old familiar knot in her stomach. She squeezed her eyes tightly shut to stop the tears and her mind was transported back 25 years, to when a 15-year-old Lorna Boyd as was, met 16-year-old Neil Smith on her parents' caravan park in Berwick. To a different time before it had all gone so wrong for her; her previous life!

Sunny View Caravan Park certainly didn't live up to its name. It was hardly ever sunny and it didn't particularly have a view; it was a former farm on the edge of Berwick with limited views as it was surrounded by woodland and fields. Lorna's dad had inherited it seven years earlier and instead of just selling the dilapidated buildings and land, in their wisdom her mam and dad had decided that they wanted to live the dream and convert it into a caravan site. Lorna and her sister Andrea were too young to understand what was happening; all they knew was that they were suddenly transported from their comfortable terraced house to a caravan where it was always cold and cramped, while the house was converted and the land made suitable for caravans to be sited.

On reflection, it wasn't a bad idea. There was a small river, well, a stream at the edge of the property, but there was good fishing and Sunny View Caravan

Park was going to be all about getting back to a simpler life. Of course it didn't work like that; people wanted a little shop that sold all the basics they would need for their stay and a gift shop and maybe a club house that held bingo nights and had the odd 'turn' on. It was an ever changing canvas and one that had her mum and dad tearing their hair out.

But over the years they got it sorted. They bought a dozen caravans out of the profits of the terraced house sale and then let the other pitches out for other caravan owners who paid fees for the privilege every year. All in all they had 30 static caravans and they had room for another 20 or 30 touring caravans or tents in the glade. In the height of season it was a busy place to be and business was good. They had their dream and they were loving their life.

She and Andrea grew up and helped out around the site for pocket money. It usually entailed cleaning out caravans, something that Lorna hated – other people's rubbish – but she put up and shut up and got on with it. All her school friends thought that it must have been amazing living on a holiday park, but the reality of it was that she and Andrea had virtually brought themselves up; her mum and dad always seemed to have something to do. Only in the winter months when the caravaners had all gone and it didn't matter so much about how quickly things were done, did the family even have chance to spend time together.

It was a good foundation for life though; at least it's what her mam always says. The things her girls learned there weren't taught in school. She was right; she wasn't expected to go and clean the school staff room or toilets every day, was she? It had its upside too though; she had pen pals all over the country, it seemed that everyone wanted to make friends with the sisters from the farm and every day the post brought news from someone. She liked writing letters and she liked receiving them. That was how she had kept in contact with Neil.

He had come to Sunny View Caravan Park with his parents one summer and the sisters had befriended the boy who always seemed to be on his own. He was from Newcastle, a place where Lorna had lots of friends; he was 16 and had just left school. Unlike any other 16-year-old she had met, Neil was shy beyond belief and at first the three of them had struggled to have a conversation. But gobby Andrea soon got through to him and before he left for home, they had exchanged addresses and promised to keep in touch.

Andrea wouldn't write; she never did. A year younger than Lorna, she was very much a here and now person; she only saw what was under her nose. The minute Neil's parents had driven off the caravan site, Andrea would have forgotten about him. But not Lorna; she put his name and address in her little notebook and sent off a letter saying she hoped he had enjoyed his holiday and had had a safe journey home. Meticulous even in her letter writing, she did as she always did and put the date she had sent the letter next to his name. Some people never replied. Lorna would keep them in her notebook for a while, but eventually she would put a line through the name and address and not bother writing again.

Neil had replied by return post. It had been the

beginning of a long and committed correspondence, where they confided in each other about everything. They had both left school and both gone into their families' businesses; she was a glorified chalet maid; he was a trainee accountant doing day release at college. Neither of them probably doing what they really wanted; they were both short on friends and a little bit lonely. When he asked her if she would be his girlfriend she immediately said yes. It was a strange old relationship, for the first year especially. They would talk on the telephone now and then; both shy and unsure what to say, the letter writing was better, they seemed so much closer through ink than they were verbally.

It wasn't until they had been corresponding over a year did they actually physically meet up. Lorna took the bull by the horns and asked if she could go to Newcastle for the day; what could they say? She was almost 17 and apart from the odd trip out with Andrea, she didn't go far. She had never kept her blossoming romance with Neil a secret and didn't keep her rendezvous with him hidden either. She told them what train she would be leaving on and which train she would be returning back on; she would appreciate a lift to and from the station if someone could manage it!

He was waiting on the platform for her. The intervening year had seen him change from a gangly boy into a more well-built young man. Both shy at first, it didn't taken them long to overcome their awkwardness and by the time they were sitting in a burger bar eating lunch, they were chatting and laughing as if they had never been apart. They knew each other so well; they knew each other's innermost thoughts, but she couldn't take her eyes off him; physically she had forgotten what he looked like. She liked the look of him and when he kissed her on the platform as her train came in, it seemed he liked the look of her too.

Because she had managed to get to Newcastle and back safely it became a regular occurrence and their relationship continued to grow. For the next few years she would go down to Newcastle firstly for the day and then as she got older she would stay for a weekend. His family were nice and they seemed to approve of the shy girl from the Borders. By the time Neil qualified as an accountant and took a full-time position in his dad's company, they were engaged.

Lorna was still working at Sunny View Caravan Park; why would she have wanted to work anywhere else? Andrea had gone to college to train to be a hairdresser and later secured herself a job in Berwick, but Lorna had no such aspirations. She knew that sooner or later she would be moving south, so was happy to bide her time on the farm. And eventually the day came and she packed up her things into suitcases. She would miss Sunny View Caravan Park and she would miss her family. Neil was her future though and as he and his family descended into Berwick for their wedding, she was the happiest girl in the world.

Neil's parents lived and worked in the city. Their office was in the city centre but they lived in one of the suburbs in a leafy avenue. The house prices there were astronomical, so Neil and Lorna had found a lovely little house in one of the surrounding towns.

To Lorna it was like a little palace and she treated it accordingly; everything in it had its place and the whole place shone constantly like a new pin. With no friends as such, Neil and her home were her life; she thought of getting a job, but she liked having Neil's tea on the table for him when he walked through the door and to be honest she was just waiting for the day when they would hear the pitter-patter of tiny feet. Sometimes the loneliness was crippling, but she knew she would feel different when the baby arrived.

It didn't though. Every month she would think it was going to be the one, but then it would be disappointment and the wait all over again for the next month. Neil told her not to worry, it would happen when it happened, but she couldn't help but start to obsess about it. She read books and articles, time when she and Neil were intimate and then lie for hours with her feet in the air hoping against hope that that time would be the one. It wasn't and every month the disappointment was worse and worse. When her mum suggested that she paid the doctors a visit she hummed and harred; what if there was something wrong? Could she bear the disappointment?

In the end both she and Neil both went along to the appointment. Tests; more tests and then even more tests and all the while she kept hoping against hope that her monthly wouldn't arrive and all would be well. It didn't and it wasn't. Neil was fine, it was her, and in what seemed like a whirlwind, she was admitted into hospital and any hopes she had of becoming a mum were taken away from her.

The pain of not being able to ever have a family

was far worse than she could ever have imagined. She turned from a timid and shy girl into a ranting and raving lunatic. She would push and push Neil, picking fights whenever she could. Why would he want to be with her? She was barren! He deserved better. He would make a lovely dad and he was still young enough to start again with someone else. She got herself so wound up that she actually took herself off to Sunny View Caravan Park and stayed there three months, leaving a bewildered Neil behind.

She installed herself in one of the caravans and refused to hear Neil's pleas that came via her mum, to go home. She just wanted to be on her own and she wanted to give Neil the perfect excuse for him to end their marriage. He didn't though, he left her for a few weeks assured that she was okay by the daily telephone calls to Lorna's mum and dad, and then he came to see her. And he continued to come and see her until he knew she was well enough to go home with her. At first he would just come for the day and then he started coming for a night and eventually he would come straight from work on a Friday night and return straight back to work on a Monday morning. They walked and they talked, cried and ranted at whichever God had dealt them the blow. And eventually she believed him when he told her he loved her and that they would still have a good life together even if they hadn't been blessed with children.

So she went home; still fragile and likely to burst into tears or fly off the handle if she read anything about a child being abused and hurt. Why would those people be given a baby and her and Neil not? But time healed; it was still there but she could manage it. She had Neil and he was the most important person in her life and she lavished all her affection on him. He worked long hours and whereas before it didn't bother her being in the house day in day out, now that she wasn't waiting for a baby she knew she had to find something to do to take up some of the hours that he was out at the office.

She got herself a little cleaning job in the local primary school. It was just a couple of hours a night, but it gave her a purpose. Through the day she would do her own housework, shop and prepare meals and then at 2.30pm she would take the few minutes' walk to the school where she would work with another two ladies until 4.30pm. She would then return home, shower and have Neil's meal on the table for him coming home at 7pm.

It wasn't much of a job and when she had first told Neil what she was going to do he thought she was mad. A primary school? But it helped; she liked watching the little ones leave the school at the end of the night and cleaning the classrooms with the little desks and chairs gave her some sort of comfort. It would have been easy just to shut herself away, she didn't want to though. She had taken the bull by the horns and faced her demons head on and eventually it didn't hurt so much.

The money gave her a little bit of independence. She didn't need it; Neil more than provided her with everything she needed. So she saved her wages and the next time they talked about going on holiday, she paid for it. It was a liberating feeling. She liked treating Neil and from then on in it was always her money that paid for their annual holiday. It was the highlight of her year. Two weeks at a different destination around the world. Neil worked so hard, so the two weeks away were a treat and they certainly made the most of it. It was their time and even though there were never going to be any little Smiths they were strong and getting through it together.

Even when her sister Andrea gave birth to two little boys in quick succession, it didn't hurt as much as she thought it might. They were cherubs and she enjoyed seeing them; she had even had them to stay with her on occasions when Andrea needed a babysitter. She spoilt them rotten and where before she had avoided shops selling children's clothes and toys, now she would be in there buying all and sundry for the two little boys. She and Neil were even their godparents; it was the nearest they would ever get to being parents themselves and they took on the responsibility very seriously. They were the aunt and uncle that every child would want.

The years passed by. When Neil's dad retired he took over the business; at first Lorna didn't particularly notice that his days were getting longer and longer, but when it started to get to that he wasn't getting home until 9pm most nights, she had to ask what was happening. It seemed he had taken a new client on, his first without the guiding hand of his dad. Anyway, this client was demanding and everything about him and his business was complicated.

She didn't like seeing him so stressed and tired and suggested that maybe he did some work from home so that at least he could be back at a decent time, eat and then if he needed to work, he could just use his study. So that's what he did. But sometimes she would wake at 2am to find that Neil was still beavering away on his computer in his little home office. He looked dreadful and she suggested that maybe he should pass the client on to some other accountant, but he said no; he had already done so much work for him that he couldn't afford not to finish the accounts for the current business year.

And then it was over and she got Neil back. They took a lovely cruise together; Neil paid up the difference for the cost of the expensive holiday and life was good again. But within no time it started all over again; the stress, the late nights. It was a pattern that would emerge for the next four years; Lorna couldn't understand why he didn't just get rid of Charles Bainbridge and Company. But he said it was his most lucrative client and it needed his expertise to oversee all of their dealings.

Then one night he didn't come home. She rang the office and his mobile but both remained unanswered. She was beginning to panic and think that maybe he had had an accident when there was a knock on the door. It was two detectives who as gently as they could, told a frantic Lorna that her husband had been arrested and was currently at a city centre police station answering questions.

She didn't understand. What could Neil have done? He was a gentle soul and wouldn't hurt anyone! The police officers weren't very forthcoming and before she knew what was happening they were waving a warrant in her face and removing Neil's home office computer along with files and paperwork; even their personal stuff.

It was the beginning of a nightmare. She didn't

understand any of it, even when she had opportunity to see Neil she didn't understand. It took Neil's dad, Raymond, to explain why her husband was in so much trouble. And it was all to do with Charles Bainbridge who to all intents and purposes seemed to be a rogue. Raymond was furious that Neil had got involved with him; the company hadn't needed the likes of him and his dealings, but it had happened and now they were going to have to try and untangle the mess that Neil had got himself caught up in.

He was bailed, thanks to Raymond and a solicitor who cost an arm and a leg. It was a very subdued Neil who returned home. He said very little, ate little and slept even less. He was in big trouble; so was she, though for the life of her she had no idea what was going to happen. It just seemed to involve embezzling and tax evasion, both of which went over her head. They talked about custodial sentences; was he really going to go to prison? She couldn't bear to think about Neil in a prison cell; she wanted to wrap him up in cotton wool and take care of him. But he was having nothing of it and for the second time in their marriage they drifted apart; this time it was Neil who shunned her.

Her mum and dad came down. They tried to keep them both positive. Why didn't Lorna and Neil move up to Berwick and help run the site? There was plenty of work for all of them. It was a bit of hope and Lorna did her best to show Neil that there was something else for them. They might have stood to lose all of their material possessions but they still had each other; even if he went to prison it wouldn't be for long. She would go to Berwick and then when he could he could come too. Even if they lived in a caravan, what did it matter??

And he seemed to perk up a bit. The house was put on the market; there was money that was going to have to be found not only for Neil's legal team, but for the fine that if he was lucky would save him going to prison. It looked like it was going to be an enormous amount; they would lose everything Neil had worked so hard to get. They were hoping that because he wasn't a threat to society that a suspended sentence would be the worst he would be handed; he was pleading guilty; surely that would be enough. Charlie Bainbridge had been charged too, but unlike Neil there were other factors involved and he was pleading not guilty and had even indicated that he didn't know what his accountant was doing. He said basically he had handed his books over to Neil and then had signed the paperwork without knowing the ins and outs of what Neil had done!

Neil was being made a scapegoat and if Charlie Bainbridge got his way. he himself would be walking free from court and Neil would take the flack. There was no defence for Neil; he had taken on the client and had carried out creative accounting and was paid handsomely in return. All his dealings with Charlie Bainbridge had been done verbally; there were no documents or emails of instruction from Charlie; he had been much cleverer than Neil.

The business that Raymond had worked so hard to build up closed virtually overnight. People closed their accounts and took their business elsewhere; people lost their jobs and Raymond lost his reputation. Neil struggled to look his father in the eye.

He hadn't meant for any of it to happen; he had been naïve and stupid and thought that landing such a big client had been a coup, especially as it was the first Neil had brought in on his own. Luckily Raymond wouldn't lose anything; he was still a director of the company, but apart from a small pension, he no longer made any drawings. Apart from his reputation his life would stay intact, so to speak.

With nothing to do Neil became more and more subdued. He hardly left the house and there was an air of despondency about him. Lorna tried to keep things as normal as possible; she went off to work as usual; she even ignored the whispering that went on around her. Neil had been all over the papers when he had been arrested so everyone knew what was happening. When a court date was set it seemed to send him even further away from her; it was like there was an elephant in the room all of the time. They went to Berwick for a week or so; she told him all about working there; what they could do and how they could live a nice simple life. He seemed better. They wouldn't have much, she thought, but they would have each other; that was enough; that had always been enough for her. And on their return he too seemed to think that they would be okay; it would be a different life to the one they had had, but what else did they want? He seemed happier.

The week before court it was all hustle and bustle; solicitors, paperwork, the house sold which threw Lorna into a spin; what if he did go to prison? She didn't have a clue how to sort out the paperwork, lest pack the house up!! It was a chaotic time. Neil seemed to switch off; he heard what people said and did as they asked, but he didn't engage. He spent a lot of time in the garden, just sitting on the bench or mowing the lawn; it was like he was taking great big gasps of air in case he didn't get any for a long time. Sometimes he would go for a walk; Lorna would ask if he wanted company; he didn't, he just liked to go on his own. She just wanted to help; she just wanted to make the most of every minute they had together, just in case. But he shunned her just like she had done to him years earlier. What could she do?

The day before court she decided she would totally clean the house from top to bottom. Her mum, dad and Andrea were coming to stay for moral support for them both, so she spent the day hoovering and dusting. She was going to miss the house; they had spent all of their married lives there and had mostly been happy. But realistically it was a family home; that's one of the reasons they had bought it, it had plenty of room for a growing family. By the time they realised that the family was never coming they were both settled and moving seemed like a huge ordeal. It had been the right decision; the house had been a sort of comfort blanket wrapping itself around Lorna. She had never been frightened living there; not living there seemed like a very frightening thought.

Happy that the house was spick and span, she went to the kitchen and made herself a coffee. Standing looking out of the kitchen window, she wasn't fazed when the front doorbell rang; Neil often forgot to take his keys now he wasn't using his car so much. So she sped to the door, pleased that he was back in plenty of time for her family arriving; they would be a united front when the eventually arrived.

The two police officers standing on her doorstep confused her. Yes, she was Mrs Smith; yes, Neil Smith was her husband and of course they could come in! She ushered them into the living room, confused as to why they were even here; surely there hadn't been a last-minute hiccup with court the following day. They asked her to take a seat and she did, the three of them sat. What they said next would be etched on Lorna's brain for the rest of her days. A body had been found; it was believed to be that of her husband Neil Smith. There had been a wallet found; Neil's wallet. Lorna screamed. She knew she was screaming but she couldn't hear it. She couldn't see or hear anything. They had made a mistake; it couldn't have been Neil; they were selling the house and they were going to live in Berwick. He wouldn't leave her; he would never leave her...

But he had. Raymond had had to go along and identify his son's body; there was no doubt. There had been no note; no explanation. All they were left with were feelings of guilt; did it matter so much what he had done? Did it matter that he had destroyed his family's business? That they were losing their home? None of it was worth losing his life for.

Lorna got through those months in a sea of fog and tranquilisers. Her mum stayed with her; there was no way she could be left to her own devices; there wasn't a minute of the day where she was left on her own. If it wasn't her mum then it was Neil's distraught parents or Andrea; even her dad had come and stayed when her mum had had to go back to Berwick for a few days. She had wanted to follow him; she didn't want to live without him, what was there to live for? Through the post-mortem, the funeral and the inquest that followed, every action was done on some sort of auto-pilot; she was doing everything in the third person.

Every night she would wake up screaming for him; she would feel someone in the bed beside her and think it had all just been a nightmare. Satisfied that the warmth of the body next to her was Neil, she would drift off to sleep only to go through the whole scenario again an hour or so later, when the realisation that it wasn't Neil but her mum or Andrea would start the grief all over again.

Three months after Neil's death, she was still living in the house and mentally she was in no better shape. The vendors had pushed the move date back; it was the least they could do under the circumstances, but they were in rented accommodation and couldn't wait forever. The house needed to be packed up and she needed to move out. But she couldn't do it. In the end her mum bundled her into the car and drove her back to Berwick. She stayed there for two months; in the meantime the house was packed up and her furniture had been placed into storage.

Not knowing what to do with Neil's belongings, they too had been packed into crates and shipped to the storage facility along with the rest of the stuff. In Berwick, slowly but surely Lorna re-entered her life. The nightmares didn't come as often, mainly due to the amount of walking she did. She would set off first thing in the morning and walk and walk and walk.

Eventually the fog cleared to mist and on some days there were clear days; but the mist would roll in and she would be lost again. But she was no longer angry; she understood. Neil was a proud man and he had let them all down; she got that. What she didn't understand and would never forgive herself for was not seeing it. How could her husband of 15 years have suicidal thoughts in his head and she hadn't known? The guilt she felt was unbearable. She had felt glad when he had gone for a walk that morning; she had wanted to clean and he had been under her feet for days. If only she had told him not to go; that she needed him to dust the cobwebs off the ceiling or something! He wouldn't have gone; he would have stayed and helped; he never left her if she needed him. But he had gone and he had walked into the wood and climbed a tree!!!

She couldn't bear to think of the rest. What had he been thinking about? Had he been thinking of her? Had she been the last person he thought about? The thoughts went around and around in her head. She had needed him; he knew she needed him; so why had he left her??? She veered from anger to despair but at least she had started to feel. For almost six months she had felt nothing apart from abandonment; now she had a whole new set of emotions to cope with. But at least she was reacting.

Back on the bus she wiped the condensation off the window; she was nearly home. The girl listening to the music was no longer there and glancing at her watch she realised she had been on the bus for over an hour; the majority of that down memory lane. It was five years since Neil had killed himself. The reverberations were still being felt. With no one to prosecute the courts decided that the money would have to be paid out of Neil's estate. Lorna lost everything. The house had been sold, but the funds were gone and all the other assets that Neil had had were gone too. There wasn't a single penny left for Lorna. All she was left with were debts. Both hers and Neil's family wanted to clear it off, but she was having none of it and with no alternative she went bankrupt. She didn't care about the bankruptcy; she saw it as a way of drawing a line underneath her life with Neil; it was an ending of sorts.

Getting off the bus, she ran through the rain until she was at her front door. She had moved in when she returned from Berwick just in time for the first anniversary of Neil's death. Initially with nowhere to live, she had gone and stayed with Neil's mam and dad until she had sorted through the things in storage. It was a mammoth task, not least because there was so many of Neil's things amongst it; so many memories, so much hurt. But she had to be ruthless. The things in storage were all she had; some of them were quite valuable and she needed every penny she could get. So she sold the lot; she wanted nothing from her previous life; it was over and she needed to move on. In the end she ended up with quite a little nest egg, but it wouldn't last long and by the time she had paid a deposit and rent on a property, and bought herself a bit of furniture, there wouldn't be a lot left.

Raymond helped her find her little house; he had even gone guarantor when the landlord wasn't sure if she was a viable tenant. But she had got it and had been living in the little one-bedroomed house ever since. It was in the same town where she had lived with Neil, so it was bittersweet. On good days she would wander happily around the places they used to go to together; other days she would shun them. She had needed a job, but even though she had an impeccable reference from the primary school when she had left her cleaning job, it seemed that everyone knew her story and the mud that Neil had created had certainly splattered and stuck to her.

Her parents had offered to help with her finances, but she wouldn't have it. Sunny View Caravan Park was just about holding its own and there was no way they could support their widowed daughter. She lived frugally, spent hardly anything on herself and she would panic every month thinking that she wouldn't be able to pay the bills. When she saw an advert in one of the shop windows looking for someone to sell make-up door to door she thought she would give it a go. She rang the number and the lovely lady on the other end of the phone sounded very encouraging and wanted to come around and see her the next day.

Thinking that she best front up and tell her about herself before she wasted her time coming only to tell her she wasn't suitable, she gave her a quick rundown. Flabbergasted when she said it was fine, they could work around the fact she didn't have a bank account, they arranged to meet the next day; 24 hours later she was a door-to-door make-up lady. And she had made her first new friend, Nicki, who explained how she could run her 'small business', how they would get around the fact that she had no bank account. She went through all of the products, explaining what was used for what; make-up was something that Lorna obviously used, but didn't take much interest in. Now she had to take an interest; know what was for what; it was far more complicated than she could have ever imagined. But she persevered.

Nicki was an old hand; she had been doing it for years and had made her way up the make-up ladder and now had a number of ladies under her management; Lorna had no such aspirations but knew she was going to have to work at her own small piece of the business to scratch herself some kind of living.

And she had. At first clueless about how she would sell the products and gain customers. Still naturally shy, the thought of knocking on doors terrified her, but it had to be done and with brochures in arms she spent days handing them out with the promise she would return a few days later for the order. But it was slow; she would return to find that there were no orders and her first order for products was pathetic; she hardly earned a pittance. But Nicki encouraged her; told her to keep at it, that the orders would come. And she had been right; they did.

Letting herself into the house, it was warm and cosy. The heating was on low constantly; something she had thought was frivolous at first, but watching some morning television show one day they were stressing that it was the most economical way to heat a home; they were right. In the winter months her bills were much more manageable without the constant on and off. It was just one of the many ways she had learned how to keep her head above water. There was a note through the door; her latest delivery had been left in the coal-house around the back. She made her way outside before she took her coat off and collected the boxes. After all these years of being a make-up lady her orders were always large and she knew the rest of the evening would be spent dividing the orders up for her customers ready for delivery the following day.

Her life was so much different nowadays. It had been so long since she had been married to Neil living in the big house with money no object. It seemed like a lifetime ago. She missed Neil; missed the intimacy of their relationship; he had been her best friend. For years she had been angry; he had left her, but not only that, he had left her with nothing. Over the years her feelings had changed, though. Even though every day was a struggle she had found some kind of peace. She had friends, something which she had never had before; Nicki had introduced her to other make-up ladies and somehow she had managed to strike up friendships with them. She had made friends with a couple of customers; she liked it that they all called and text each other. They would have nights out in town, go for meals and the cinema and when they had realised that it was almost her 40th birthday they had arranged to have a day in York.

She was happy. In a calm and quiet way, she had made a life for herself. Still in the midst of her bankruptcy, she still struggled. The money she made off her job was erratic, some orders bigger than others, and every single penny she earned was accounted for; rarely was there anything left for treats. But she managed. If she needed anything she would save for it; her sideboard was full of tins with labels. There was one for rent; utilities; food and there was another which just said 'Lorna' and that was where she kept her little bits of money. She was forever in it taking out to top up the other tins, but at the minute there was enough in for her birthday outing; not quite as much as she had hoped thanks to her bad management with regard of the train tickets, but there was enough for her to have a grand day out in York.

She made herself a cup of coffee and a sandwich; the boxes of orders were in the middle of her living room floor and she sat with them while she ate her sandwich. She was looking forward to the weekend; York on Saturday and then she was going up to Berwick for a few days on Sunday afternoon. She still saw her family a lot; Sunny View Caravan Park was once again thriving, mainly thanks to the credit crunch and the need for people to holiday at home instead of flying out to the Costas and stuff at astronomical prices. 'The Costas!' They always made her think of Neil; not because they had often holidayed there but because of Charlie Bainbridge. He had been found not guilty and had walked away from court and straight onto an aeroplane to the Costa del Sol and was never seen again. He had dragged Neil's name through the court and in his absence the court had believed that it was all Neil Smith's doing and Charlie Bainbridge was free.

But it was water under the bridge. She had to look forward and not back. Her mum and dad had booked for them all to go out for a meal on Sunday evening; Andrea, her partner Robert and the boys. It would be a good night.

When Lorna went downstairs the following morning all of the orders she had placed into bags were standing in a uniform fashion on her little dining room table. Every row of bags was a different street and she was going to try and get as many of them delivered that day along with the new brochures so she could collect the orders in and have them sorted before the weekend.

As she waited for the kettle to boil for her morning coffee she pulled her little shopping trolley out of the cupboard; it was the only way she could deliver the orders; and she was now a regular sight in the area walking the streets with her shopping trolley behind her. Half an hour later she was ready to go with her first run of orders; she had made herself a kitty of change and her shopping trolley was packed to the rim.

By mid-morning she was doing well; most people had been in and she only had a couple that she would have to go back to later in the day. Her next drop was her friend Jackie's house. They had struck up a great friendship over the years and she was one of her friends that was going to York with her at the weekend. The door was open so giving a cheery, 'Ding dong!' she made her way in, leaving her shopping trolley in the hallway.

Lorna did wonder if Jackie really needed the continuous orders she placed, or did she just feel sorry for her? Nevertheless, she made her way into the kitchen where Jackie was already pouring water into the coffee cups. They chatted for the next half hour; mainly about what they were wearing on Saturday depending on what the weather was like first. She handed her £8.96 order and in return Jackie produced a £20 note. Handing over her change including £10 note HE75 229564, she kissed her on the cheek and left to continue on with her deliveries, with the promise she would see her first thing Saturday morning.

Back at the house she scoured the cupboards for something for lunch. There wasn't much; she never had much in. Deciding on a boiled egg, she set about preparing it. Boiled eggs were one of the millions of things that reminded her of Neil; he loved a boiled egg in a morning and she had learned to perfect them to just the way he liked them. Spoon in hand, she smashed it down on the little white egg in the egg cup; the yolk splattered everywhere. Anger spent. She put her head on her dining room table and sobbed...

14

They Know the Cost of Everything

and the Value of Nothing

The front door closed behind Lorna; Jackie, sitting at her kitchen table, continued to stare at it as if it was going to spring open again. Sighing, she picked up her order off the kitchen table and took it upstairs to put at the bottom of the wardrobe along with many other orders she had bought from her friend over the years. Every now and then she would remove a bubble bath or a shampoo; but even if she never bought another item from Lorna again she had enough of everything to last her for years. Lorna's instinct had been right; Jackie only placed an order every month because she felt sorry for the woman.

Lorna had never said much about her life, especially her 'previous life' as she called it. But Jackie knew; nearly everyone knew her tragic story and that was the reason that when she had come knocking on the door, all apologetic and frankly terrified, she had taken the brochure and placed her first order. And she hadn't stopped since. Gradually they had become friends, but Jackie didn't ask, she hadn't needed to. Her youngest, Billy, was still at the primary school where Lorna had worked when the news broke in the newspapers. The lovely woman with the faint Scottish accent, who always had a hello for her and Billy when they passed at the end of the school day, was a hot topic of conversation around the school gates.

Even when Lorna no longer worked there, Jackie had followed the story in the press and was shocked and angered when she had read that Neil Smith had hung himself in a nearby woodland. The poor woman. So when she had turned up on Jackie's doorstep a year or so later, she had recognised her straightaway and took pity on her.

She liked Lorna, she liked her a lot and was looking forward to having a day out with her the following weekend. There was a whole group of them going and she hoped that it would take Lorna a little bit out of herself; she always looked like she had the worries of the world on her shoulder. And to be frank, when she had found out she was about to celebrate her 40th birthday, she had been shocked. For some reason she thought she as older; maybe that was because she didn't really make the best of herself; life seemed to have trodden her down. But at least she had an excuse to dress up on Saturday; she might even drop in before that and see what she was wearing. She had talked the talk earlier in the day, but chances were that Lorna would turn up in her usual attire of jeans and jumper. Jackie wanted her to have the wow factor; something she guessed she hadn't had in a long time. She made herself a mental note to call on Thursday at some point and see her, at least that way she had a chance to sort her out; even give her something of her own to wear if need be.

But Thursday was a million miles away and she had so much else to do before then. Her afternoon was going to be spent answering telephone messages and emails; there was a charity function at the Town Hall that evening that she was attending. Tomorrow would be taken up with meetings; as was her Thursday morning and then on Thursday afternoon she held her monthly surgery. She might get a chance to call and see Lorna after that!

She had little idea what she was taking on when she had decided she would run as a town councillor. It was certainly a beast that needed feeding continuously. It was something she had even planned to do, she sort of just fell into it; but she was now in her second term so she was either a sucker for punishment or was actually quite good at it and felt like she was actually making a difference. She liked to think it was the latter; her door was always open, so to speak, and she made sure she always had time for the people she represented. Mostly it was an uphill battle; the establishment was very well established and she was still thought of as a bit of an upstart. They didn't say this to her, but she could tell by her fellow councillors' roll of the eyes when she had something to say, that they thought she shouldn't be there; it wasn't a job for a nearing middle-aged woman. But she was going nowhere and God willing, she would be running again next time.

Jackie Newell was 43 years old. Mother of two;

Dean who was 18 and Becka who was about to turn 15. She had been married to Jack for 10 years, largely due to the fact that she was still married to her first husband when she had met Jack 20 years earlier, but five years and two kids later he had finally made an honest woman of her. Jack and Jackie Newell – their friends all called them Jack and Jack. It might have taken them a while to get round to getting married, but they had known as soon as they had met that they were perfect for each other.

She had been lucky; she knew that and that was one of the reasons why she had decided to become a town councillor; not quite a Prime Minister, but if she could make a small difference in the area she lived in and made it better for people to live there, then she was happy. She had just never thought for one moment how much work it would actually involve and how much organising she had to do, especially having two demanding teenage children.

But Jack helped; he didn't mind moving the kids from here to there when she was tied up with her work. He didn't mind people knocking at the door ranting about their wheelie bin not being collected or that there was no grit in the bin around the corner. He would just usher them into the little front room which they had converted into a kind of office for Jackie, and offer them a cup of tea.

It had all started at primary school where Lorna used to work. Becka was in her final year there but still liked her mam to walk her to school; even though she was more than capable of making the five-minute walk herself. Jackie hadn't worked since the children had come along so didn't mind taking her, it got her dressed in a morning or else she was sure that she would be one of those women who lived in her dressing gown. Anyway one morning as they were approaching the school gates a little girl darted out from two parked cars and was almost run over by a car coming along the street. If the car hadn't been driving so slowly there was no way it would have stopped in time and the outcome didn't bear thinking about.

Jackie was furious; it wasn't the girl's poor mother's fault; she was pushing a smaller child in a pushchair and was looking for a bigger gap so she could get pushchair through. Her little girl had just darted out, probably recognising another child on the other side of the road. Anyway all was well that time, but next time a child might not be so lucky. It was the same every morning and every evening; there were cars parked everywhere. There was just about room for a car to get down the middle of them, anything bigger than a car had no chance. Something had to be done about it. And it became Jackie's mission.

She made telephone calls; consulted with the school; drew up a petition and badgered the council constantly. For months it was all Jackie thought about. All she wanted were some double yellow lines or some of those zigzag things outside the school gates. How hard was that? But it seemed it was hard and any lesser person would have given up. But not Jackie Newell. She continued with her onslaught; letters, emails, telephone calls. She was like a dog with a bone. But what if it had been Becka? Next time it might be!

And then one day she got a letter. The council were going to put chevrons and double yellow lines on the road outside the school gates. She had won. By the time it was done Becka no longer attended the primary school, but it didn't matter, there were plenty of other children who did. She was so proud of herself for not giving up; a small victory but a win nonetheless. And it had given her a taste for it.

She had decided that when Becka went to secondary school and was settled she was going to go back to work. It wasn't particularly about the money, Jack was on a good wage as a supervisor at a local factory, but it was the thought of living in her dressing gown day in and day out that spurred her on. It turned out to be harder than she thought. Before she had the kids she had worked as a purchase ledger clerk in an office. But that had been almost 20 years earlier and technology had moved on and had really left Jackie behind, even though she could email and text and use various software packages as well as the rest of them. Even to her, her curriculum vitae looked old-fashioned. It was one of Becka's friends' mams who worked at the town hall, suggested she should maybe run as a town councillor at the forthcoming elections. She had done a great job with the school so that would stand her in good stead with the locals who would be voting.

Jackie knew little about local politics, less about being a councillor, but it was an option and one she talked to Jack in length about. She did some research; there was no pay as such, but she would be paid a basic allowance and expenses and if she sat on various panels she would be paid for that too. She didn't need to be affiliated with any particular political party, she could stand as an independent and that clinched it for her, that and Becka and Dean's approval. It would have an effect on them too if she was elected. They seemed to think it was a big adventure and as soon as she decided she was going to stand and did all the relevant paperwork, their house became like something in an American presidential election. Bunting, posters, all courtesy of Becka and Dean and their computer know-how.

Knocking on people's doors was difficult at first; she felt like she was bullshitting people to vote for her, but then she got into her stride. She shouldn't be telling the electors about her; she needed to listen to them. She would take a note of their names and addresses and write down any grievances they had. Mostly they were all about the same sort of things. Fortnightly wheelie bin collections; litter; parking; the threaten closure of the local park and the library; gritters in winter; grass cutting in summer; policing or lack of police; parking; Council Tax. The list went on and on. But Jackie persevered. If she was elected then at least she would have something to start on immediately.

By the end of her campaigning she was really starting to enjoy herself. She liked meeting people; Jack warned her not to be too disappointed if she didn't win, they had started very late on the election trail and there was some stiff completion from the major political parties' candidates; and there was always next time. But she kept on; even on polling day she had arranged to pick voters up and take them to the polling station. She stressed over and over to them that it didn't matter if they didn't vote for her; she just didn't want them to not use the vote that their forefathers and foremothers had fought so hard to get.

By the time voting closed at 10pm she was exhausted. But there was still the count and the results to get through before she could even think about going home and putting her feet up. As they walked into the Town Hall Chambers the place was packed. There were so many wards in the area, her ward being one of the bigger ones, and therefore it would be less likely that the count would come in quickly. The four of them sat on a table and sipped at tepid tea; it was a late night for the kids, but how often did your mam stand as a councillor? There could be exceptions to bedtimes sometimes; even on a school night.

The Chambers seemed to be getting fuller and fuller; people kept coming over and wishing her luck and she mainly gave them the same retort: maybe not this time but she would certainly be standing again next time.

And then the results of her ward were in and they were being ushered onto the small stage. It was all very formal and ceremonious and to be honest she didn't really understand what they were saying. Even when they were saying which candidate had what vote, she couldn't hold the figure in her head; as soon as they mentioned another name she lost the count of the one before. And then they were saying her name, Jackie Newell, 35,902. Was that good or bad? She had no idea; she couldn't even remember what the demographics for the area were. She should know, she looked at them often enough! Her brain had turned to mush.

Then she heard her name being mentioned again and there was lots of whooping and people were cuddling her and shaking her hand. She looked at Jack and the kids standing behind her. Jack must have realised that she was lost and came straight across to wrap his arms around her. 'You won, Jackie, or should I say Councillor Newell!' She couldn't believe it. She had only been in the running for a few months; she didn't stand for any party, just for herself and she had damn well gone and won it.

She was delighted and proud and apprehensive and very scared. But for the next few weeks she floated around on some sort of cloud. She organised a monthly surgery and attended her first few meetings, where she found it difficult to even open her mouth and say anything. But like anything, she got used to it and slowly but surely she started to understand how the Council worked; the red tape, the bigotry of some of the more senior councillors who seemed to run their wards with blinkers on. She knew as sure as eggs were eggs she would have run-ins with them and she was right. There were many battles.

But she listened to her constituents and she did her best; sometimes she had success, other times not. She stopped one of the parks being sold for housing but couldn't hold back the library closure. She had the library bus brought in a couple of times a week, but it was no replacement for the little library and she felt that she had let her people down. But there were other smaller victories over the years. Flowers were planted all over the town and a new memorial was built for all the men and women who had fallen in the wars. But these were only superficial victories.

There were bigger issues that over the years she would champion but she wouldn't change a single thing about it. She couldn't have done it without the support and understanding of Jack and the kids. Sometimes the whole thing took over her life and she would disappear into her office for hours on end firing off emails, letters and making telephone calls.

She met all sorts of people from all walks of life. Sometimes she would thank God for her lucky stars for hers and her lot, the life they shared as well as the love; she didn't know such poverty existed right underneath her nose. Some people lived such desperate lives – money; relationships. She thought nothing else could shock her and then something else would come along and even if it wasn't what they were seeing her about, things would come up in conversations and she would wonder how they managed to put one foot in front of the other. It amazed her how resilient people were and how much they tolerated.

The charity function she was attending later in the day was for victims of domestic violence. One of her big passions over the years was the availability of a refuge for such women and children. It had been a long hard slog, not just for her but the charity that had championed it. But a building had been made available and the money raised by the fundraiser would go some way to providing fixtures and fittings, with the hope that it would be able to open in the coming months. She thought she might ask Lorna to get involved; she might enjoy doing a bit of voluntary work and made another mental note to ask her.

The afternoon was spent mainly doing what she set out to do. She made her telephone call, typed up about a dozen letters and then started on her email.

One in particular caught her eye, it was from the planning committee at Town Hall – one of the many committees she found herself sitting on; it was the bane of her life. There were about a dozen reports and spreadsheets attached to it and she thought it would be easier printing the whole lot off and then having a read through.

It was all to do with some wasteland that was to be the first phase of the council's new housing policy where they were building affordable housing along with a splattering of houses that would specifically be used to top up the council's depleted housing stock. It had been years in the pipeline but at last things were moving and this was the first draft of phase one and the outline for phase two, both of which would be completed in the next three years. It was very exciting; it had been over 30 years since any new housing had been built. The first phase alone was for 75 houses; a mixture of room sizes and layouts. Laying the plans on the desk, she read the accompanying report and spreadsheets.

Confused, she read and re-read the report. The spreadsheets confirmed what she had read in the report. All the costings were there, all broken down into the smallest overhead, but there must have been some mistake. It had been agreed that there would be a 55/20 split; 55 houses which would be sold and 20 that the council would rent to suitable tenants. The reports showed that there were to be 70 for re-sale and only five to rent; how had that happened?

Jackie was absolutely furious, it had been agreed that the development would only go ahead if there were at least 20 rentable houses in each phase. She rang a fellow committee member; he as green as she was. There had been no mention at the last sub-committee meeting either. She fired off an email to the chairman, a not particularly pleasant one but one that very much got her point across; in short she told him that he and his committee members might have known the cost of everything but the value of nothing. There were families on the housing list that had been earmarked for the rented housing because they had been in either inadequate housing or in privately rented accommodation; 20 families had been selected and now there were only five houses. She stated that she was appealing against the plans and was sure that she would generate enough interest from fellow councillors and the press if need be. Livid that money had been put before a duty of care, she switched off her computer and stomped upstairs to get ready for her evening out. She couldn't get it off her mind though; how had this happened? At what point did they make the decision to potentially dump 30 houses and sell them off for profit over the two-phase build? The tenders had gone out; builders had been shortlisted! It all beggared belief. Something was nagging in her mind and she couldn't shake it, but it was a throwback to the 70s when the councillors were in the back pocket of builders. Corruption. She wouldn't let it go; she wouldn't. She would fight.

By the time she jumped into her friend Lucy's car she had calmed down. Lucy worked for the Citizens Advice Bureau and they had become quite good friends over the past couple of years. Lucy was the person that Jackie would go to when things were a bit out of the box or she needed a bit of advice. They were both strong supporters of the women's refuge and were looking forward to the night ahead. It made a nice change for them both to have the opportunity to dress up and as they parked the car and walked towards the Town Hall they both received admiring glances from people walking by. They were a sight for sore eyes!

Walking up the steps someone caught Jackie's eyes. A young lad was sitting on the steps, obviously a down and out; one of many she had seen sitting there over the years. He was young, maybe late teens and even without seeing him close up, he looked resigned and forlorn. Jackie's heart went out to him. He didn't look much older than Dean; how had he ended up here like this? She thought to herself, *Drugs? Alcohol?* He didn't look like an addict; he just looked lost. On an impulse Jackie did something she never usually did. Opening her handbag she grabbed a £10 note and made her way over to him.

Up close he looked even worse; her heart contracted. He was just one of many, they slipped through the net and ended up doing God knows what just to survive. At least tonight he could get himself some food, she thought to herself as she handed over £10, HE75 229564, and told him to go and eat. Grateful, he smiled the biggest smile and thanked her. Turning, she made her way back towards Lucy who was standing on the steps waiting for her. 'Soft touch!' she said, smiling at her.

'He could be mine, Lucy! And it's only £10!!!' Pushing open the door, they walked together into the glittering reception area where a waitress handed them both a flute of champagne! It was just £10.

15

Show Me the Money

K ai watched the lady walk up the steps and go and meet another woman who had waited for her. He knew the Town Hall steps would prove lucrative; he had seen all the balloons and stuff being taken in earlier in the day and thought there must me a posh do on. Sometimes if he hung around outside long enough he would get lucky and someone would drop him a couple of quid; if it didn't work on the way in then he would sit around until they came back out. He didn't have anywhere else he needed to be and they were usually a bit more generous when their belly was filled with beer.

He had struck gold in the first half an hour; a tenner – he would be able to have himself something to eat and still have some left over for some cigs. He decided that he would sit there a bit longer. The people were starting to flow up the steps and he was sure that if he stayed sitting he would be good for a few more quid. He was right; by the time that he made his way down the steps he had almost £20 in his pocket, bolstered by the kind lady and her £10 note.

He had been living rough for almost three months, but had been away from home for almost six. For the first few months he had squatted in a property in the city centre; it had been rough but okay; at least there was a roof over his head. He had even managed to get himself a little job; just collecting glasses in a pub, but the money helped. He could eat and keep himself clean and tidy. It was hard sharing a house with so many people; some nights there would be as many as twenty sleeping there; it was impossible to stop your belongings from being stolen unless you carried them everywhere with you. In the end, apart from a few quid in his pocket he had nothing left to steal.

And eventually he lost his job; he didn't have the money to replace his clothes or to keep buying soap and shampoo; in no time he started to look grubby and no matter how many showers he had, without soap he started to smell and no one wants to employ someone whose hygiene is in question. So his only means of income was to beg and steal.

When he had run away from home he had never expected it to be as hard as it turned out to be. He hadn't really known what to expect. But living rough and begging had never been something that he thought would be an option. Maybe he thought that the street would be paved with gold and they were just waiting for him to come along. He couldn't remember what he had been thinking; all he knew was home was a long, long way away. It wasn't; as the crow flies it was maybe 10 miles, 15 by road, but it was far enough for him not to bump into anyone he knew; even if he did Kai doubted that they would even recognise him; he hardy recognised himself anymore. He looked like what he was – a tramp!

Nothing horrific had happened to make him leave home; he wasn't abused or beaten. It was just a never ending round of arguments with his mam and dad; he had wanted to spread his wings and they wouldn't let him. Every day was a battle, until one day he packed up his stuff and left. That had been almost seven months ago and he hadn't been back. He had wanted to, loads of times, but it was like he had passed the point of no return and he didn't know how to even go about it. He knew him being missing would be making his parents ill; they had no doubt been frantic when he just didn't come back from school one tea time; they had probably searched and searched. But he had gone straight into the city where you could be invisible if you wanted to and even though people questioned him about why he was there and where he came from, no one really cared.

When the squat had been emptied by the police there had been nowhere else for him to go. The city was a very different place after dark; every doorway had occupants huddled against the biting cold night air; usually the same people went back to the same place over and over again. For a 15-year-old boy it was a dangerous place and even if he eventually found somewhere that he could put his head down, he had to sleep with one eye open.

So he moved himself out to the suburbs. There weren't as many homeless there and there were more opportunities to not only beg but to do a bit of pilfering too. It didn't bother him, stealing. Sometimes he would shoplift; sometimes he would break into houses; working alone, he could be in and out without drawing suspicion. He wasn't scared; maybe his thinking was that if he was caught, then the police would find out who he was and call his mam and dad. It was a win-win situation for him.

If he broke into a house, it was usually just food and a bit of clothing he stole, he had little use for anything else. It was no good stealing electrical goods or jewellery, he had nowhere to sell them. So he just stuck to practical stuff. His best steal had actually been a sleeping bag; he clung on to it as if his life depended on it, which it did. He tended to go to the same spot every night; it was sheltered and no one bothered him. Through the day he would hide the sleeping bag close to his hidey hole and pray no one stole it.

Sometimes the nights were never ending. Often falling quickly to sleep, the slightest sound would wake him and he would lie in the dark and listen to the sounds of the night. That was the time he wanted to be at home in his own bed with his mam and dad sleeping close by in the next room. He would lie in his sleeping bag and the thoughts would run around and around in his head. He would promise himself that he would ring home the next day and he would fall back to sleep with the image of pizza and chips and burritos and a red hot shower in his head. By the time he woke, his courage would have left him.

He didn't like to think too much about the people at home; his mam and dad, his nan, his friends even. He had left in a moment of madness, not really thinking about the consequences of his actions. He was a 15-year-old living alone on the streets; apart from the people he had met at the squat and at the pub he had spoken to no one, especially now he was living in a town. No one saw him. His life was the complete opposite to what it had been at home. There he had been, the centre of everything; his mam and dad had doted on him; they ferried him to football and friends' houses and whereas at the time he thought they were trying to control him, now he saw it was because they cared and wanted to keep him safe. Out on the streets no one cared.

When Kai was born he had a twin brother, Luke. They were identical, there were pictures of them both and he would wonder how his mam and dad had could even tell them apart. Then at nine months old Luke hadn't woken up. Obviously Kai had no memory of Luke, but knew that he was the reason that his mam and dad tried to wrap him up in cotton wool. He resented Luke so much for dying, sometimes he had even wished it had been him that had died. He had no life so it may as well have been. But he could see now why they were like that; why they were scared to let him go into the shopping centre with his mates or the pictures or even stay at a friend's house. They were scared they would lose him. And he had done all of this to them. He had walked out of their lives and as far as they were concerned they didn't know if he was alive or dead.

He walked off the Town Hall steps and made for a café he sometimes went into when he had a bit of cash. The lights were on and he could smell something that smelt like his mam's broth when he opened the door. Walking to the counter he saw the girl look him up and down; he knew he looked a mess and she probably thought he was going to ask for something for nothing. He was right, there was a big notice advertising a bowl of broth and dumplings with a slice of bread and a cup of tea for £3. He would have that and then he would have egg and chips; £5.65 in total. He ordered his food politely, but the girl stood looking at him. 'Show me the money!' her expression said. Digging into his jeans pocket he took out the £10, HE75 229564, that the lady going into the Town Hall had given him. Satisfied that he could pay, she took his money and handed him his change. Beckoning him to go to a table, he moved to a table near the back of the café next to the window.

No sooner had he sat down than the girl had brought him his broth and his mug of tea; there were four slices of bread. Smiling, she told him it was nearly closing time and she had a couple of slices to spare. He thanked her and started on his food straight away. He was starving. He had always been a bit of a fussy eater at home; his mam would make him stuff and he would turn his nose up. Now he ate anything. The broth was hot but tasty and in no time it was gone along with the bread. As he waited for his egg and chips to come he looked around the café; it was almost empty, just an old couple sharing a pot of tea.

Looking out of the window he realised that it was already dark. The cars parked outside had condensation on them and it looked like it was going to be a cold night. He shivered; the cold damp nights were the worst. The slugs would come out and he would wake in the morning to find himself surrounded by them; they made him feel sick and he hated them. The thought of a night in his sleeping bag filled him with dread, but at least he would have a full belly and he would call at a little shop on the way back 'home' to buy some cigarettes. At least when he woke in the middle of the night he could have one of them to calm his nerves.

His egg and chips arrived along with more slices of bread; they must have been throwing a whole loaf out. This time the girl said nothing but he smiled at her in thanks. It was all delicious and once again it was gone in minutes. A fresh mug of tea arrived along with some jam roly poly and custard; before she even had chance to say anything Kai laughingly said, 'Was it going to waste?' And she walked away laughing. Twice that day he had met kind ladies; they made him think about his mam. She was kind, she was always lovely to his friends; nothing was ever a bother. It wasn't for his dad either. They were good people, he just hadn't seen it.

He sat for another half an hour or so; the girl had started to put the chairs on top of the tables and he knew that she wanted to close up. He carried his dishes to the counter and thanked her again. She said it was fine and she was pleased he had enjoyed it. And then he left. The wind had started to whip up and he was right, it was going to be a cold night.

Undecided about what he was going to do, he made his way back to the Town Hall and sat on the steps. Some of the guests might start coming out early, he thought to himself; he still had a few quid left, but opportunities like this didn't come along every day so thought he best stick it out and see what he could get.

He must have been sitting there about an hour when he saw the £10 note lady come out with her friend. He couldn't hope to get anything more out of her, but he watched her make her way down the steps. There was something about her that reminded him of his mam and all at once he wanted to cry. What was he doing? Why was he living like this when he had no real need to? The lady was down the steps and walking away from the Town Hall; he could still remember her kind face from earlier in the day. He was up and running down the steps before he could stop himself. He couldn't drag his eyes off her, he was just so frightened that he would lose sight of her.

She must have heard his footsteps coming along behind her because she turned just as he got to her. 'Missus, missus!' he shouted. She looked startled and a little bit frightened as she saw who it was chasing after her shouting. 'Please, missus, can you help me? Can you ring my mam for me please…?'

16

Cross My Palm

The boy was young, very young; maybe not as young as he actually looked, but still too young to be out on the streets. When he had first come into the café she was sure he was going to ask for some leftovers, but he hadn't, he had shown her the colour of his money and ordered his food. Her heart had gone out to him; she wanted to ask him why he had ended up living rough. Where was his family? His friends? She hadn't; she had took his money and if he had thought to check he would have realised that instead of it costing him £6 it had just cost him £1; she had deliberately put in his hand a wad of coins hoping that he would just put it in his pocket and not check.

Emma watched him wolf down his broth and bread as she plated up his egg and chips. It must have burnt his mouth but he didn't seem to notice; he was scruffy but he thought that given a good bath and haircut he would be a fine-looking lad. She buttered him more bread and stole a look at the time on the wall clock; ten minutes until closing time. She was going to be late closing.

The elderly couple left and there was just her and the boy left in the café; while he ate his food she piled up a bowl of pudding for him. It was just going to go to waste and he may as well have it; he certainly looked like he needed it. She could tidy up and close around him, so that was what she did. By the time the boy stood up to go she had most things done and it would only take a few more minutes for her to have the place ship shape and ready for Mrs Baker arriving in the morning to re-open in time for breakfast.

The boy thanked her before he left; she smiled at him and told him it was fine before shutting the door, turning the sign to closed and turning the key. For the next five minutes she washed the boy's dishes, swept the floor and made sure that everything was switched off and the surfaces were clean.

Emma Keeps had worked in the small backstreet café for 18 months; it was one of two part-time jobs she had. Every weekday afternoon she would arrive at the café for her 3pm shift; Mrs Baker would leave and then Emma would look after the café until it closed at 7pm. It suited her fine; she had a hearty meal when she was there and Mrs Baker always paid her more than the minimum wage that she should have really been on. Weekends she worked in one of the city centre clubs; just on the bar, but they were long hours and sometimes she wondered if she should just take Mrs Baker up on her offer and work weekends for her! But seven days a week in the café was not an attractive proposition; at least in the bar she mixed with people her own age and if her friends were out she would sometimes meet up with them for a couple of hours before some of the more hardcore clubs closed

Neither of her jobs were taxing; the money was okay and because she still lived at home with her mam the money was mainly her own. Both of her employers were understanding when she needed to take time off; sometimes weeks because she very much had other irons in the fire. She had left school and gone straight to drama school; that was her passion and any opportunity she got she would act. Everyone told her that she was good; she had always had rave reviews about her performances; but opportunity was limited and she was still waiting for her big break.

Her mam had said that she was born singing and dancing; one of those little girls who liked nothing more than constantly being in the limelight. At the age of four years old she had started at dance school, and hadn't stopped. She loved performing and had always been sure that it was something that she not only would make a career out of, but would make her famous. But it had alluded her; she had auditioned for so many parts but apart from a couple of local productions and of course a few seasons of pantomime as the principal lead's stand-in, it hadn't happened!

It hadn't happened until eight weeks ago when she had received a telephone call off one of the producers she had worked with on a production of My Fair Lady. He asked if she could go to his office because he had heard that there was a part in a television programme he thought she would be perfect for and wanted her to audition. At 25 it was the first time that someone had actually asked her to audition for a television part. She was so excited and couldn't get around to Paul's office quick enough.

There was indeed a part; but it was all very hush-hush. It was for a very well-known serial drama set in London; the part was for a young Geordie girl who would turn up as one of the main characters' long-lost daughter. Discretion was everything. It was to be an explosive storyline and if the press got wind of the character arriving it would spoil the plotline. Of course she was interested; the character was supposed to be about 22, but she could play a 22-year-old; she looked barely 20 herself. Happy that she would give it a go, Paul made a couple of phone calls, said he would send the producers an email and would confirm if and when she had been selected for interview.

Emma was so excited. Nothing like this had ever happened to her before; she had a flair for accents, but it seemed that she would be auditioning in her native tongue. This was the break she had been waiting for; the one that would fire her into superstardom. Paul rang a couple of days later; yes, she had been selected and they wanted her to audition in London the following week.

She had never auditioned for television before, never mind been in front of a camera, and she spent any spare time she had not only researching that, but also the programme. Even though she was an avid viewer she needed to look into its archives to see where the character she was auditioning for could have been conceived. Happy, by the time she got on the train at Central Station bound for London, she was ready.

The whole thing was nothing like she had

expected. She had thought she would be going to the famous studios, but the auditions were being held in a London hotel; what she hadn't been expecting were the volumes of girls that were there auditioning just like herself. Not normally nervous, her tummy had birds flapping about in it; butterflies were too small and insignificant for the feelings she had going on.

She waited hours for her slot. By the time she actually got into the room she had fed the birds and she was back in her usual calm state. She kept saying to herself, 'This is your big chance, Emma. This is your big chance. Don't blow it!' And she didn't think she had. She had followed instructions and had read the script they had set out. She finished. There was no round of applause; just silence. They thanked her and told her they would be in touch in due course. And that was that.

Making her way north on the train, she looked back on her audition and picked it apart. She could have put more feeling here, maybe toned down that bit there, and maybe using her own accent was a mistake; maybe she should have put a softer lilt to it. It was done though and there was nothing she could do now but wait.

She had waited and waited. She had expected to hear something within the first week but there had been no news. Paul hadn't heard anything either; the best he could gleam was that the producers still hadn't made a decision. She was like a cat on a hot tin roof, jumping every time her mobile rang. But there was nothing.

Now it was eight weeks since her audition. She hadn't heard a peep and she was just so pleased she hadn't told anyone about it; not even her mam. It was obvious that she hadn't got the part; surely if they had wanted her they would have snapped her up before someone else did. But there had been no other parts; she hadn't even looked, so sure had she been that she would get the one in London. Her confidence in her ability had taken a huge knock.

Happy that everything was as it should be in the café, she took the money out of the till, totalled it up and put it into the cash tin that would then be hidden in the kitchen ready for Mrs Baker coming in in the morning. Putting on her coat and collecting her handbag, she was annoyed at herself for not thinking that she needed change for the bus fare home before she had put the cash tin away. Retrieving it, she took a £20 note out of her purse and changed it in the tin for £10 – £5 and five £1 coins. Dropping the cash into her purse, including £10, HE75 229564, she put the cash tin back into its hiding place and locked up the café.

It was a cold and miserable night and her thoughts went again to the young boy who would be sleeping rough in it. Her own warm bed had never seemed so tempting. She hoped he saw sense and changed his life; the alternative didn't bear thinking about. By the time the bus arrived she was freezing, but the bus was packed and there was the horrible smell of wet bodies; a bit like wet dogs. Finding a seat near the back of the bus, a sudden wave of something she had never felt before engulfed her. Despondency? She wasn't sure; she just had the feeling that maybe this was her lot! There were no bright lights waiting for her; not stardom or at least a bit of recognition for her talent. She felt sad! She had never felt sad before and she didn't like it. She should never have auditioned for something so big; she should have just stuck at what she was doing in the hope that one day someone would see her worth! She had set herself up for failure; it had been a mistake.

Opening the front door, she could hear laughter. She had forgotten all about her mam having her friends over; it was the last thing she felt like. They would ask her if she had been discovered yet and they would laugh. She had known her mam's friends all of her life; they had watched her as a young precocious child and then a confident teenager and the drama queen she had turned into as an adult. And they had laughed. At her; with her. There had been no malice meant by them; they were northern women who called it how it was. Maybe she should take a leaf out of their book and see things how they were.

She was a failed actress. Luckily she hadn't gone in search of fame, but even so she had to admit that it probably wasn't going to happen for her now; she was too old. She also knew she couldn't carry on working in the bar and café forever, she would have to get herself a job where at least she would get some sort of job satisfaction and she needed to get herself a place of her own; she couldn't stay with her mam forever. There was a need for change.

Putting on her biggest smile, she made her way into the kitchen where her mam and her friends were sitting. They all had a glass of wine in front of them and when her mam handed her a glass she poured herself one and sat down next to them. For the next ten minutes she was bombarded with questions. No, no acting job; no, no boyfriends. She really didn't have a lot going for her, she thought to herself as she took a big gulp of wine.

When the living room door opened and Shirley, her mam's oldest friend appeared and her mam disappeared, the penny dropped. They were all here because her mam had booked a fortune teller. For the next few minutes she sat listening to Shirley amazing the others with the things that Madame Zita had told her. Things that she couldn't possibly have known. Emma thought it was all mumbo jumbo and they had more money than sense.

Her mam came out and amazed them all over again! By the time she had been amazed by four of these women Emma's curiosity was piqued! Maybe Madam Zita had some idea about what direction her life was taking. Yes, her mam said; there was room for her to see Madam Zita if she wanted; £15 cheap at half the price. But she would have to wait to go in last. Taking her coat and shoes upstairs, she checked her emails – none of any interest – and then quickly changed out of her work clothes and into a pair of leggings and jumper. She had only just started to thaw out and there was a distinct smell of wet dog about her.

Back downstairs; another friend had been told something that was putting a huge smile on her face. Not wanting to ask what all the commotion was about, Emma poured herself another glass of wine and waited for the next person to come out. Then it was her turn.

She felt nervous. What if there was something about this fortune-telling malarkey? What if she told her that this was as good as it was ever going to get for her? What then? She was sceptical; what could a stranger know about her and her future? Her mam and her friends might have been taken in by what Madam Zita had said but they must have been giving her signals and answering leading questions. Well she was an actress and she wouldn't give anything away! Let's see what the fabulous Madam Zita could get out of her. It was a waste of her hard-worked-for £15, but she would give her a chance; it would be a laugh if nothing else. *Let's see if Madam Zita is a better actress than I am,* Emma thought to herself as she opened the familiar door of her living room and made her way in.

Madam Zita was nothing like she had expected her to be. About 30 years old, she wasn't dressed as Gypsy Rose-Lee; she was dressed similar to Emma. Wearing her deadpan face, she sat down opposite Madam Zita as she continued to shuffle the tarot cards in her hand before handing them to Emma, asking if she would be kind enough to give them a shuffle too. Emma was taken aback by the lilt in her voice; it had traces of an Irish accent but it was mainly Geordie, but with a sing-song edge to it. Satisfied that she had shuffled the huge cards enough without dropping them, she handed them back.

'Cross my palm, sweetie!' Madam Zita said. Emma dug out the cash she had put in her jumper pocket earlier and handed it over; £15 in notes including £10, HE75 229564, that she had changed at the café earlier. Madam Zita placed the money to her side and taking the pack of tarot cards divided them into three piles. Indicating to Emma to choose a pile, she reshuffled them and then in what she could only describe as of a bit of a frenzy, Madam Zita laid the cards on the table in some sort of pagan pattern.

Emma was fascinated. Madam Zita seemed to be concentrating really hard on the cards and her eyebrows rose up and down and sometimes her nose turned up as if in disgust. She waited patiently to be amazed, but Madam Zita didn't seem satisfied with what the cards showed; she then picked the two discarded piles up, handed them back across the table to her and asked her to shuffle again.

She had to concentrate hard to re-shuffle the cards; although there was now less of them, they were just so big. When she was happy that her job was done she handed them back to Madam Zita, who once again split the pack into three and Emma had to choose again. Then it was more of the same; turning cards, raised eyebrows and upturning nose! The whole process fascinated Emma and she had to concentrate really hard to keep her deadpan face in place.

The Madam Zita began. Emma was determined she wasn't going to give anything away and would just listen and not be led into answering questions! 'Well I can see that you are an only child. There are no men in your life. There's a James here; he had been passed a long time, but he says that he watches you with interest!'

A shiver ran down her spine; she was spot on so far; she was an only child and there were no men in her life. There was no dad, hadn't been for years, and no boyfriends. No uncles or cousins even. If she thought about it, the only men in her life were people she only knew as acquaintances. She wasn't sure about James; but hadn't her granddad being called Jimmy? How strange, she thought to herself; she knew all of this from just a few pictured cards. She had her full attention now as Madam Zita went on:-

'I can see you aren't happy with your lot. James is saying he can see you surrounded by cups and glasses. Does that mean anything to you?' When Emma wasn't forthcoming she started saying names of people and Emma really wasn't sure who she was talking about. But then she said something that really grabbed her attention. 'I wasn't sure if the cards were playing with the first spread. That's why I asked you to do it again. And since James is here he has put some light on the matter. I have another lady here; James says that she is his aunt so I'm supposing she must be your great-great aunt. Anyway, she has been passed for the longest time. She is here now and she is dancing around behind you!' Emma resisted the urge to turn around. She had no idea who this lady could be!

Undeterred, Madam Zita went on. 'The lady is telling me that she was in the music halls when she was young; she says she is the same as you or you are the same as her! She is still dancing; so is James!' Looking Emma directly in the eye, she said, 'That's what you are going to be, isn't it?' Dumbstruck, she continued to sit. Had Madam Zita recognised her from one of her theatre productions? She doubted it; she didn't look like the type who would sit through a pantomime or a production of Macbeth.

'I see stars. There are so many of them floating around your head. But there are question marks too. Is there something you are waiting for the answer to regarding your acting?' Emma tried not to react, but this was all just too unbelievable; how could she possibly know?? She nodded quickly! Madam Zita smiled; handing her the tarot cards that she had disregarded earlier, she asked her to shuffle them again. This time they weren't so awkward in her hands; even though they had started to shake. Once again satisfied that she had done a good job, she handed them back across the table.

This time Madam Zita spread the cards fan like in her hands. 'Concentrate really hard on the cards. When you feel you are drawn to one card then pick it out and hand it face-down to me!'

She looked very hard at the cards in Madam Zita's hand. Never believing for one minute that any one of them would jump out at her, they all looked the same, she concentrated just like Madam Zita had said. And then it happened. Her eyes kept being drawn to one particular card within the pack. Tentatively, she took hold of the card and handed it face-down to Madam Zita; just like she had told her to do.

She was holding her breath; she knew she was but there wasn't anything she could do about it. She had asked the question and maybe the answer was on the turning of the card. Any scepticism she had was well and truly out of the window; the deadpan face had long since slipped.

Madam Zita turned the card so it could only be seen by her. 'I think I know what your question was and is about. You wanted to know if you were going to get your lucky break.' She laid the card down on the table. Emma couldn't quite see what it was, but there seemed to be stars on it. Her tummy did flips. Madam Zita continued. 'Ten of Pentacles! I'll tell you the interpretation of the card and you can tell me if it is relevant or if you need it explaining further! If your success is focussed on material wealth (career, money, status, possessions), the Ten of Pentacles shows that you will have what you desire. You are surrounded by the financial rewards for your labour and you feel secure in this success. That is what the card means! Does that answer your question?'

Emma was totally, totally speechless. She stared at Madam Zita as if she was an alien that had just landed in the middle of her living room. How on earth could she know? The card meant success and recognition and of course money. She had asked if she would get the part she had auditioned for and if she did, would she be successful at it. She had her answer; if Madam Zita was to be believed. Yes, the cards had said. It didn't matter how long it took for them to get in touch with her; the part was hers. Madam Zita and her cards had predicted that she Emma Lewis was the next big thing on the BBC. A star was about to be born!!!

17

Money for Old Rope

Madam Zita bundled up her belongings and put them into her handbag, along with the £150 she had made from her night's work. Obviously she wasn't really a Madam; she wasn't Zita either. She was plain old Jean Carson; but her real name didn't have the same allure as Madam Zita.

She bade her goodnights and left the house. She had parked her car around the corner; it never did to roll up in her Range Rover for readings; it would give the totally wrong impression. If they thought she had come on the bus they were more likely to believe that she was a real Romany Gypsy; well, maybe not as much as pulling up with a horse and caravan, but still image was everything and she didn't want people to know that she was actually quite well off.

Pulling the car away from the kerb, she made her way down the street, pulling the bobble out of her hair and letting it tumble around her shoulders. Even if any of the ladies she had just given readings to saw her now, they wouldn't recognise her; no one ever saw her as Madam Zita when her hair was down; with it down she was just Jean.

It had been a good night; she felt like they had all had value for money; especially that last one, she was a one to watch. She wished she had asked her name or maybe got her autograph, it was going to be worth something in a year or so. It was funny, the rest of the night she had winged it, nothing was particularly coming through and she was having to use all her skills of observation just to gleam something that would help her gain their confidence. But when the girl that came in last go into the room it all happened naturally, the spirits came: the old man and the all singing all dancing lady; the cards were readable and she knew without a shadow of a doubt that this girl was something else.

Turning her car towards the town centre, she decided that she would go and give her husband Eddie a hand closing up. They owned two amusement arcades, one in the town and the other in the city centre. The bigger one in the city closed early; it was far too much like hard work handling the drunks that found their way in after dark. But the town centre one didn't close until ten; it was a much more sedate affair, usually full of pensioners playing bingo and on the one-armed bandits. They still got the odd drunk, but they were few and far between.

She had been married to Eddie since she was 17; less an arranged marriage and more an arrangement. He was her cousin, not a real one; his mammy and daddy had always been her aunt and uncle and vice versa. If there was blood there, neither family knew anything about it. It was just one of those things when two couples were close and there little ones came along, they were always called auntie and uncle. Eddie was two years older than her and from being little she had followed him everywhere, much to his annoyance. But she didn't stay a gangly little girl forever and by the time she was 15, the ugly duckling had grown into a swan. Eddie never twisted about her again.

Both families' roots were in Ireland, but Jean had never been; her whole family had moved to England before she was even born. There had been no reason for her to go and she had never had any fancy for seeing the 'old country'! Eddie still had people out there; he had often retuned with his brothers and later with their sons, but it held no appeal; she was English and learning about her roots held no appeal. She was a much more 'here and now' type of woman.

She and Eddie had had a good marriage. They had been blessed with three sons and later, when they thought their baby days were over, they had had a daughter. She was the apple of everyone's eye and spoilt rotten. At 18, she was beginning to be a worry with her wayward ways, but she had plenty of people keeping an eye on her, so Jean tried not to worry too much. Jean and Eddie worked hard; they had done well for themselves, but it had come with its own problems. For years they had put up with being called names in the street; 'scrounging Paddy bastards' was a favourite, as was 'pikey'. But they had both learned a long time ago if Irish is what they wanted then Irish was what they got. There might have been name calling but people that didn't know them were wary of them and tended to give them a wide berth; it suited Jean fine.

In fact it was because of the aura that Jean supposedly gave off that she became Madam Zita. If people were going to be a bit in awe of her, she may as well cash in on it. She wasn't the seventh daughter of a seventh daughter; she was actually the only daughter of an only daughter of an only daughter! Nothing special about her at all. But her granny had had second sight; her mammy hadn't but even as a little girl Jean saw things that other people didn't. She had the gift, her mammy would say, but she didn't want it, she just wanted to be normal. So she ignored it, even when her granny had sat her down and told her she couldn't ignore it; she had. The only time she had paid any attention to it was when she had set her cap at Eddie Carson; then she would listen to the whispering in her ear, the little voices telling her that he was the one. And of course they had been right. Or had they? Was it that she had just grown up into a bit of a looker and Eddie had noticed her? Or that both sets of parents were keen for them to get together, cement the families so to speak?

As she got older, the more she would listen to the voices. Sometimes they would be there all of the time; other times they would just come to her in her dreams. Sometimes she saw them, other times they were just shadows. They didn't frighten her; they didn't want to hurt her; they just wanted to help.

When they first got married before the children came along, she and Eddie ran a burger van. It was hard work and they seemed to always be hitching and unhitching the converted caravan off the back of their car. But the money was good and they travelled around all over the country selling their wares at fairs and shows. The biggest one, besides Appleby fair, was The Hoppings at Newcastle's Town Moor. It lasted a week and it was one of the most lucrative times of the burger van year.

One particular year they were parked beside the fabulous gypsy caravans; each was more lavish and garish than the next and Jean was fascinated by the queues of people who would stand for hours to have their palms read in the hope that their future was going to be better than their passed. All the 'gypsies' were real old-school and had an aura of mystique about them that made her stare whenever they nipped across to the burger van for a portion of chips or just some change. But the one thing she did notice; they made good money.

By the end of the week, her curiosity was unbearable; not just to see inside one of the beautiful caravans, but to see what the fuss was all about. She would hear people chattering in the queue as they waited to be served their burgers; some had the same stories – they were going to have a win, the man of their dreams was just around the corner, they were going to have two children, one boy and one girl. And so it would go on. Jean was intrigued. Every now and again there would be one of the little voices in her head saying, 'No, she isn't having a win, in fact she is going to lose her purse and be out of pocket!' Were the gypsies real? Were the voices and people she saw? There was only one way to find out and that was to take the bull by the horns and go and see one of them for herself!

She decided on Gypsy Morag Lee; according to the blurb on the caravan window she was a seventh generation clairvoyant with two lines of Celtic blood coursing through her veins. There were a number of photographs of her with B-list celebrities, but if the queue outside her caravan was any indication of her talents, then Gypsy Morag Lee was the woman for her.

Jean was first in the queue when Gypsy Morag Lee opened her caravan door. Dressed in her day clothes and her hair falling down around her shoulders instead of its usual working bun, she resembled nothing of the woman that fried burgers in the snack van opposite the gleaming caravan.

Inside was impressive. Everything was mirrors and porcelain, every shelf was jam-packed with figurines of ladies; the mirror effect made it look like there were even more of them. The whole place was gleaming like a new pin and she wondered if anyone actually lived there or if the caravan was just used as a place of business! Jean found the whole thing a bit creepy but followed Gypsy Morag Lee to the front of her caravan, where candles burnt and the table held a crystal ball and a deck of tarot cards.

Gypsy Morag Lee asked what type of reading Jean wanted. Puzzled, the gypsy went on to say palm reading, tarot or crystal ball. Unsure, she said cards and then was told to cross the gypsy's palm with the relevant amount of cash.

Fascinated, she watched as the gypsy shuffled the deck of cards and then handed them over for Jean to shuffle too. After a few minutes of clumsy shuffling, the cards were returned to Gypsy Morag Lee and she divided them into three packs, from which Jean was asked to choose one. The other piles disregarded, she then laid the cards out on the table and studied them hard. Silence. She picked up the pile of unused cards and asked her to shuffle them again; same procedure again and once again she said nothing.

'I'm not getting anything, my lovely, the cards aren't being kind. Maybe you have the gift too! Yes?'

Jean wasn't sure what she should say. 'I hear voices and sometimes see things, but I don't think I can do predictions!'

The older lady stood and went to the area which was a small kitchen. She made two cups of tea and returned to the seating area, passing one of the cups to Jean. For the next 30 minutes they chatted about what Jean could do and basically what she could do with it. Gypsy Morag Lee explained that even she couldn't read for everyone, sometimes she had to just guess. She said she became very good at people watching, looking for signs like wedding and engagement rings, black eyes around the eyes usually indicated babies and so on and so forth. Her gift, she went on to say, was 70% guesswork and 30% skill. Jean was flabbergasted. It was a con! The whole prediction thing was made up of guessing games and something she hadn't thought of herself, eavesdropping.

Gypsy Morag Lee said that she gleamed more information about people standing in the queue than any other source. She said they all talked; if you listened hard enough you could hear what they were hoping would be predicted and like a domino effect, if she got the first one of the day right, then they would go outside and talk to the next in the queue and then the next client would let slip what it was they were hoping to hear.

Sometimes the spirits did come through to guide her, but not often. Like with Jean, the spirits had come, but they had been laughing and didn't want to talk. Gypsy Morag Lee had seen it before, they did that when she was being made a fool of and unbeknown to Jean, she was much better at predictions that Gypsy Morag Lee could ever hope to be. She handed Jean her £10 note back and told her that one day she would find a use for her gift. It wasn't a prediction, she said, it was a fact.

Years later, after the boys were born, the burger van was set on fire by a rival vender. Eddie, in his haste ran to try and limit the damage. It was too late for the van, Eddie burnt his hands badly trying to put out the flames and the once flush Carson family were down on their luck. Obviously there had been no insurance on the burger van; Eddie couldn't work so it was down to Jean and a conversation she had had with old Gypsy Morag Lee years earlier. It was time that Madam Zita came out of the shadows and into her own.

And she saved the day. She had written little post cards and placed them in shops around the area advertising Madam Zita and her predictions for the future. Taking on board what Gypsy Morag Lee had said, she advertised as 'Fortune Telling Parties' knowing that if there was a group of people, they would talk. She practised and practised with her tarot cards and much to her own amazement became quite proficient in them. By the time the first booking came in, she was ready!

It was actually money for old rope. Sometimes it was guesswork, other times the cards helped and often there were spirits to guide her. She even shocked herself how good she was. People crossed her palm and usually she would leave the party over £100 richer for just a few hours' work. And the bookings just kept on coming, she actually had a waiting list. Soon the Carsons were back on their feet. Eddie looked after the boys most nights and on a few afternoons a week, she would don her Madam Zita mask and go fill the coffers.

When Eddie was given the chance to buy an amusement arcade in the city centre from an old friend, they had the money available and took his hand off. It was a money-making machine, hard work and they constantly had to have eyes in the back of their heads, but worth it. And it was just as well. Jean was pregnant again, something she hadn't foreseen happening, and she had to step off the gas a bit with her 'fortune telling' business and instead chose to sit in the little kiosk and give people their change.

After three strapping boys, tiny Kitty was a shock. She might have been little but she was loud and demanding and Jean had to virtually give up work altogether to care for Katherine Mary-Anne Carson and her diva ways and for a few years there was no Madam Zita, just one-armed bandits and bingo when she could. But she missed Madam Zita!

They bought a second amusement arcade and life was good for them all. They had a beautiful house just out of the city centre, which now that the boys had all left home was big for her, Eddie and Kitty, but she loved it and couldn't think of living anywhere else. When the boys had gone into the 'family business' Jean had more time on her hands and decided that she would revive Madam Zita. The bookings came in and in no time at all her diary was once again full and her nights were spent reading tarots and giving people hope.

But like Gypsy Morag Lee, the majority of her predictions were guesswork. A mark on the finger where a wedding ring had once been, an overheard conversation whilst she 'got herself ready' all helped. She would ask leading questions, she would watch people's faces for a reaction, even if they thought they were giving nothing away, the usually were. She honed her skills and her reputation grew and with it the bundles of cash she made.

Every now and again, the spirits would come and that made her job a whole lot easier, or the cards would make sense. She didn't like to think she was a con woman, which she ultimately thought she was the majority of the time. She liked to think of herself as providing a vital service; people needed hope and they needed comfort. She had regulars, clients who would book her over and over again. She couldn't be all bad could she?

She parked her car right outside the arcade. At that time of night the street was quiet; apart from the arcade there were only a couple of fast-food shops with their lights still shining. It was Eddie's shift at the other shop, but that would have closed a few hours ago and he would have made his way to the other shop to help Kitty close up. She could see Eddie's car and further up the street, Kitty's. Jean smiled; she would have been furious she couldn't have got parked directly outside the arcade earlier in the day when the street would have been busy with shoppers.

Kitty was now 18 years old and as spoilt and diva-ish as she had been as a baby. With little ambition, she had to be virtually forced into the arcade otherwise she would be happy to do nothing but take money off whoever she could get it from and while away her days in the city centre or the Metrocentre. She had got away with it for a while, but then Eddie had come down on her like a ton of bricks; she needed to learn the value of money, of spending a day at work and being paid for it. With Kitty it was easy come, easy go.

She was up to something, Jean could sense it. She could sense it as a mother, not as a clairvoyant; for some reason her own family tended to remain closed books to her, no matter how hard she tried to glean information. There was something Kitty was hiding and for the life of her she didn't know what.

But it would come out eventually, time would no doubt tell. Bounding into the arcade, she found it free of customers and both Eddie and Kitty emptying the machines ready to cash up for the night. For the next hour they all mucked in and balanced up the day's takings. It had been a good day and between the two shops and the proceeds brought in by Madam Zita, they had made a pretty profit.

Securing the building, the three of them went their separate ways with Eddie instructed that he had to call and pick up a takeaway for them to have when they got home. Kitty was still sitting in her car when Jean pulled passed her, jabbering away in some heated conversation on her mobile phone. Just by her body language, Jean could tell her daughter was annoyed about something or something the person on the other end of the telephone was saying. She thought about pulling over to the kerb and waiting for her, but that would no doubt cause a strop so she carried on and arrived home a good half an hour before Eddie and Kitty.

The table was set for the three of them by the time Eddie arrived with the takeaway. Kitty was fast on his heels. When Eddie arrived back in the kitchen after putting the day's takings into safekeeping, the food was on the table and she and Kitty were already sat down and tucking in. It was a pleasant enough supper, they all had stories to tell about their day's events; Kitty was especially interested in her mammy's reading for the young actress; the family knew of old that anything Jean told them with regard to Madam Zita was confidential and so she knew that she was on safe ground telling them about the young starlet.

Kitty was fascinated; she asked Jean question after question. Did she know what show she was going on? Was she very pretty? Would she go to Hollywood? The questions went on and on. Answering them best she could, she told Kitty, 'Yes, she was pretty, the show was a well-known soap opera that Kitty herself watched and no, she couldn't see Hollywood but she would become a household name and no, before she asked she didn't know what her name was!'

Eddie laughed at them both. 'You're like a couple of old fish wives, you two are!' he said, laughing and getting up from the table, no doubt going to claim the television remote control and the length of the sofa.

Jean cleared up while Kitty remained at the table fiddling on her mobile phone. They chatted away whilst she loaded the dish washer and made herself a cup of coffee. She liked it when they spent a bit of time together doing nothing. Kitty was always in such a hurry; she rushed to work, rushed back, rushed to get ready and rushed to get out again. Sitting still at the kitchen table was a rare occurrence these days but one that Jean cherished.

Kitty was a pretty girl, she was small and petite and had inherited her daddy's titian-coloured hair. She seemed popular, had an abundance of friends who she spent a lot of time with, but there hadn't been a serious boyfriend for some time, not that Jean knew of anyway. She hadn't brought any lads home apart from the ones she had been to school with and still moved in her circle of friends. Jean had heard her talking about Jimmy. She had said a couple of times that she was meeting him after work, but he had never materialised at either the arcade or at home. Kitty was keeping him very much under wraps and that worried her.

What will be will be! Jean thought to herself as she plonked herself down in front of Kitty at the table. She had never been an interfering mammy; if Kitty had something to say she would say it, Jean trying to prise information out of her daughter wouldn't work. It was Kitty's day off the next day and she usually went out when she had a free day the next day, but Kitty was showing no sign of rushing off to get ready. Surprisingly she told her that she was just going to have an early night, she wanted to be up early in the morning. Jean stayed sitting at the table after Kitty had scampered off to her room. It wasn't like Kitty to miss the opportunity to have a late night out and a long lie in. The concerns were back in her head. But Kitty seemed happy enough, maybe she was just starting to grow up! Since she had left school she had been a bit of a party animal; maybe she had burned herself out? Jean kicked herself that she couldn't read anything about her loved ones.

Her mobile beeped. A text – Kitty! 'Can u lend me some money til payday mammy pls?'

'How much?'

'£100 if u can!'

She had only been upstairs five minutes. *Why didn't she just ask me before she went up?* Jean thought to herself. 'I'll leave it in the kitchen drawer for you!' she texted back. It wasn't a problem, Jean still had her night's takings in her handbag and she would make sure she deducted the money off Kitty's wage when she put them up at the end of the month. She was just puzzled why she hadn't actually asked her to her face. She usually did.

She washed up her coffee cup and went in search of her handbag. Finding it in the hall, she went back into the kitchen and counted £100 out. Included in the bundle was £10, HE75 229564. She put the money in the drawer, grabbed a bottle of white wine out of the fridge with a couple of glasses and went to join Eddie watching the news in the living room.

Eddie smiled his lovely smile at her as she walked in and lifted his legs so she could snuggle down next to him. She chastised herself for worrying about things that there was no need to worry about. Pouring the wine, she handed Eddie his and moved into the space his dangling legs had made for her. Snuggling down next to her Eddie, she knew that she was a lucky woman; she had a husband she loved, four wonderful children, a beautiful house and in her heart of hearts knew whatever it was Kitty was keeping from them, they would cope. If only she could see what it was!!

18

More Money Than Sense

At 7am the following morning the alarm on Kitty Carson's mobile went off. She hated early mornings and kept hitting the snooze button until it was way past half past and she decided she best get up. An hour later she was showered and dressed and drinking fruit juice in the kitchen. Her mammy and daddy had already left for the arcades; her mammy always covered her shifts on her day off and her daddy would be at the city centre one along with one of her brothers. There were so many hours to cover in both shops, but between them they managed to work respectable hours and have a couple of days off a week, though they could be changed at a moment notice.

She liked working at the arcade. At first she had kicked and screamed, she didn't want to work and she certainly didn't want to work in one of the dumps they called arcades. Used to just having to ask for money whenever she needed it, she took it badly when they fell hard on her and set her a small allowance every week. Their reasoning was that if she wasn't prepared to work for it, then she could only expect to get a small amount to spend on herself; pocket money really. Even her brothers who she could usually wrap around her little finger were having none of it. She had no choice. It was work or poverty, well, her form of poverty where she had no money for clothes or nights out. It wasn't as if her family would let her starve, but even so, it was a shock to her usually pampered lifestyle. So she chose to work. And shock of shock, she loved it.

Kitty was spoilt, she knew she was. There was a seven-year age gap between her and her next brother; she had come along as somewhat as a surprise and how they all loved her. And she loved each and every one of them back. They would say she was their little ray of sunshine. She was, she was a happy little girl, mostly anyway; given to tantrums if she didn't get her own way, but she soon got wise to that. If she was sweetness and light she was more than likely to get what she wanted than jumping up and down on the spot and screaming.

So she became a little bit more cunning and a lot more charming. School proved to be difficult, the label of 'pikey' or 'gippo' plagued her every day, but she never reacted. If they wanted to call her names then that was fine, she was the one who had the best of everything, new shoes every term, new winter coat instead of hand-me-downs like a lot of the girls that called her names. And eventually it would only be one or two of them that kept up the name calling, with others she was liked and popular.

She didn't have the gift like her mammy did; it was a disappointment to her, it would have proved helpful through her school years. She had tried, her mammy had helped her, but it wasn't to be. But still having a 'fortune teller' for a mammy had its own advantages. People were never very cruel to her, they were never sure what her mammy was capable of doing. She had a circle of good friends, both boys and girls and all of whom were happy to spend time with her at the family home. They had the latest in everything; TVs, CDs, DVDs, there was always food in the fridge and cupboard and her mammy, daddy and brothers always made them all welcome.

Her first boyfriend, Kyle, proved to be a disappointment. He had been one of her closest friends since primary school, they went everywhere together and was a regular visitor at her home. When they were about 15 years old things began to change. The usual happy-go-lucky Kyle started to be grumpy and bad tempered. It went on for weeks and weeks; they all still hung out together but Kyle started to act like an idiot, drinking, smoking, playing truant from school. He was turning into a bad lad before Kitty's eyes and she didn't know what to do about him.

When one day he texted her asking to meet him, she thought nothing of it and went straight off to the arranged rendezvous point. Kyle was drunk. He told her he was acting the way he was because he was confused, he said he loved her. Flattered, he was a looker, she said she loved him too. They became boyfriend and girlfriend. Kyle calmed down; it had seemed he had been struggling with his feelings for Kitty for months and now they were a couple, old Kyle was back.

But as relationships went, Kitty wasn't happy.

They never took things too far but she knew the first time he kissed her, properly kissed her that was, that he wasn't the boy for her and she had made a mistake. She was in it though, Kitty and Kyle were a couple and rightly or wrongly, she didn't want to hurt him. Their friends called them 'Special Ks' but there was nothing special about their relationship, not for her anyway. So she stuck at it hoping that something would switch on inside her and she would want him as much as he wanted her.

She held off getting too physical, knowing if the kissing wasn't working then taking it to the next stage was going to be disastrous too. Taking advice from one of her brothers' wives, she ended it. By then Kyle was older and if anything even better looking. She told him he wouldn't be on his own long and he wasn't. They went their separate ways as Kitty and Kyle on the Friday; by the Monday there was Ruby and Kyle. All the months of not wanting to hurt him had been ill founded; he was a teenage boy and if one girl didn't love him then there was always another who would. They stayed friends. He was still one of her very best friends and when she met Jimmy, Kyle was one of the first people she told about the relationship.

When she left school her mammy and daddy left her to her own devices for about six months. She was adamant that she wasn't going into the arcades, so they told her to look for a job she would want to do. She looked for about two weeks and then gave up. If her mammy and daddy were going to give her money for doing nothing then why work? But it hadn't worked out like that and she found herself doing her first shift and the town centre arcade.

For the first few weeks she hated it. She hated that she had to be dragged out of her bed every morning to go and open the shop. Kitty was learning from the bottom up, the way her brothers had. But she found she liked chatting to the customers; they all had stories to tell and Kitty liked nothing better than listening to other people's lives. And if the truth be known, she liked having structure to her days and a wage packet that she had earned at the end of the week.

Surprisingly she was good at the job. The customers liked her and she was forever coming up with ideas to get the customers through the doors and onto the machines. Her mammy and daddy were delighted and after about a year, she was virtually running the town centre smaller arcade on her own.

She partied hard with her friends and there wasn't enough room in her wardrobes for all of the clothes she bought. She had a girly holiday in Ibiza, much to her own surprise when she had asked her mammy and daddy if it was okay that she went. If they were nervous about their 17-year-old daughter going on her first holiday alone, they didn't show it and even took her and her two friends to the airport. It turned out to be the one of the best weeks of her life. She was free of the constraints of the family and the hundreds of pairs of eyes she thought were always watching her. She got drunk every night and much to her disgust, she had a one-night stand she remembered nothing about the following day. Her cherry had been popped and apart from a vague recollection of a boy who looked a bit like Will Young, she remembered nothing about it.

She had relished the week though and had hoped it was the first of many holidays to come. Back home she learned to drive, flew through her driving test and was rewarded for all her hard work with her own car. Life was good. And it got even better the day that Jimmy walked into the shop. It was love at first sight. Her mammy had always told her that she had fallen in love with her daddy the first time she saw him, but she hadn't believed her. Until Jimmy.

Back in the kitchen she fished the money her mammy had left her out of the drawer. Opening her purse, she placed them biggest note at back and smaller coming forward. £10 note HE75 229564 was stacked neatly in front of some £20s and behind other £10 and £5 notes. Satisfied that she now had enough cash, she snapped shut her purse, placed it into her handbag and made for the front door, setting the house alarm as she went. Her appointment was 10am in the city centre and she didn't want to be late.

As it was she had loads of time, so much time she could go and have a cup of coffee and touch up her make-up before she went around the corner in good time for 10am. Her mammy was right to think that she was hiding something; she was. In fact she was hiding two things – Jimmy, and today she was getting her first tattoo. Her mammy and daddy would go mad on both counts. Firstly for being silly enough for getting a tattoo, then for what the tattoo actually was and then on top of that they would hit the roof when they found out about Jimmy.

She had an idea on the tattoo she wanted, she had seen it on the tattooist's Facebook page and loved it; hers would be a little different though, she wanted the initials J and K entwined. She could see it now embedded between her shoulder blades. She was serious about Jimmy and she wanted the world to know it. Well, maybe not her mammy and daddy, but once it was done there was little they could do about it.

Just like there was nothing they could do about Jimmy. She had fallen in love and that was that. They could like it or lump it; Jimmy completed her. Since meeting she had never felt more alive, more loved or more assured about herself and her life. She just needed to convince her mammy and daddy that Jimmy was her soulmate.

Checking her make-up in the toilet mirrors and satisfied that she was looking good, she made her way out of the shop and around the corner to where Tats for Tarts was situated. Opening the door she saw Jimmy was already there waiting for her. She needed her hand holding and while she explained to Lola, the tattoo artist, what it was exactly she wanted, Jimmy sketched it onto a piece of tracing paper and handed the finished drawing to Lola.

For the next four hours Kitty lay on a bed and yelped and laughed while Lola did her work. It hurt and it tickled and sometimes she wanted to shout, 'Stop!' But Jimmy held her hand and when it got too much she could feel the pressure on her hand tighten. As she lay there she prayed to whatever God you prayed to when you wanted something so badly. She prayed that her mammy and daddy would see that Jimmy made her happy, that it didn't matter and that at the end of the day it was Kitty's happiness that should be their main concern. And then it was over and Lola was rubbing some sort of soothing oil all over her back. Helping Kitty stand she handed her a mirror so she could see her reflection in the larger mirror behind her. It was perfect. It was exactly what she had wanted. Lola covered the tattoo with cling film and taped it down to protect it.

Kitty felt liberated as she dug in her bag for her purse. It was really the first time she had done something that she knew her mammy and daddy wouldn't approve of. But no doubt it would only be the first of many. In her head she heard her daddy say, 'You have more money than sense, young lady!' He was probably right. She handed over £210 including the £10, HE75 229564, to Lola and then turned and smiled her biggest smile at Jimmy.

Her beautiful Jimmy. Jemima Louise Watson, also known as Jimmy Watson. Her girlfriend. Grabbing Jimmy's hand she made for the door. The tattoo was the first thing, now for the second. As they walked towards the city centre arcade her tummy did somersaults. Kitty Carson loved Jimmy Watson; everyone was just going to have to get used to it.

19

Love of Money is the Root of All Evil

Lola was pleased with how young Kitty's tattoo had turned out. She had done it freehand and she had added a lot of extra detail into it, though they probably wouldn't be able to see it clearly until the tattoo had healed. They were an odd couple. Kitty was very sweet and girly and Jimmy looked more like a boy than most boys, but very, very handsome if a girl could be described that way.

She had done quite a bit of work on Jimmy over the last year or so. She was quite artistic and would bring designs into the shop that she wanted placing on various parts of her body. Lola had to admit though, the girl certainly had an eye for it. She wondered if she would maybe do some designs for her to have in her portfolio. Surprising though, the one that Kitty had chosen was one that Lola had designed herself. If she said so herself though, it looked stunning nestled between the pale-coloured skin between Kitty's shoulder blades.

Lola still had a busy day ahead of her, at least six hours tattooing and then she had paperwork and some cashing up to do. She was having to close the shop up for maybe two weeks whilst she attended Jury Service. The timing of it was terrible, just as it had been the year before when she had to defer it as she was about to launch her shop. But this time when she got the calling there was no deferment option and she was having to turn customers away while she went and sat in a court room with another 11 good men.

Tats for Tarts was her brainchild. She had been a tattoo artist for almost 20 years and had always worked in mainstream shops. In the beginning tattoos had been mainly a man's domain, but more recently it was the ladies that were leading the way with regard to sales. And it was Lola they were asking for, not because she was better than her male counterparts, in many cases she wasn't. But they preferred to have a woman touch them than a man, especially when the tattoo they were having was being sited in a delicate place.

It set alarm bells ringing in Lola's head. There was money to be made, a lot of money. Instead of picking up her measly wage at the end of the week, she could be making money for herself. It would be a leap of faith, she had seen shops open all the time and then just as quickly close. It was the more established shops that were holding their own and making money. Would the ladies come if she made it exclusive to them? Her bank didn't think so, they weren't prepared to give her a business loan, neither was the next bank or the next one she went visiting with her business plan. They all said the same thing; she was halving her chances of getting customers through the door because she was only serving females. One stroppy young business manager virtually called her a sexist. She was furious, how dare he say that? She was wanting to make ladies feel comfortable. She wasn't stopping men coming into the shop, she just wanted a place where ladies could come, take off their clothes without them being under pressure.

It wasn't going to happen. No one was prepared to take a chance on her. Whether it was because she was a bit out of sorts at work or because he genuinely cared about her, one night at closing time her boss, Thumper, asked if he could have a word. He was a big brute of a man, every surface was covered in ink work, he was a walking advertisement for his shop. The nickname he had been given as a young man was nothing to do with him having a reputation for going around thumping people; it was because he was like Thumper from the Bambi film, soft and lovely.

Lola had worked for Thumper for five years, since her last little boy had started school. He was a good boss and understood that sometimes she had to be other places doing other things. She was a bit perplexed about what she had done wrong; he had never specifically asked to see her on her own before. But what was the worst that could happen? If he sacked her she would just go all out to get her own place, by hook or by crook. And that was the reason he wanted to talk to her; he had heard about her plans. She was so embarrassed, she had been stupid, she should have known that word would get out. She had even been to look at premises that might be suitable.

Thumper surprised her though, he said he thought it was a really good idea. Could he have a look at her business plan? She said she would bring one into work the next day, which she did and then Thumper surprised her even further by saying that he would lend her the money. Obviously he was a business man and there would be interest to pay on the loan. But he liked the idea and they could work together; he would send her ladies until she had made a name for herself and she could send any male clientele to him. She couldn't believe it. Tats for Tarts was going to happen. She could have kissed him, in fact she did.

And he was as good as his word. A loan agreement was drawn up and the money was placed into her bank account. She dropped her hours to part-time while she sorted out her own business. The downside was that during those months, apart from sleeping there, she was hardly ever at home. But it would be worth it once the shop was open. Her husband Anthony was a complete brick. He sorted out the house and the boys and still managed to go to work; she couldn't have done it without him.

It was funny because everyone thought that Lola was a lesbian. More than likely because of her appearance – she had tattoos, wild hair which was often shaved up the sides and was always in a variety of different colours, and she had loads of piercings. But she had never even had that type of tendency never mind had a relationship. She had met Anthony at university where she was studying art and he was studying economics and they had clicked. When he returned to his hometown after they had graduated she thought that would be it, but it hadn't been. Anthony had been home for about a year, they had managed to see each other now and again but then he surprised her by securing a job in the North East and asked her not only to move in with him but marry him. She couldn't have been happier.

They might have looked like the odd couple, he was as sedate as she was wild, Anthony didn't even have his ear pierced and the thought of having a tattoo himself was as alien to him as it would be for her to put a suit on and go and work in finance. They were very much together. The birth of their sons sealed their happiness. Tommy and Billy were born within two years of each other and now at 10 years old and 11 years old they looked like twins. No one looking at her would believe her, but home with her fella and her boys was where she was happiest. She loved being a wife and a mam, but she was also proud of Tats for Tarts too.

Just over a year after opening, it was doing really well. Thumper was as good as his word and sent the ladies around to her when she first opened. Thanks to her website she had got the message out that she was there and now she ran a bookings service, there was very little chance of anyone walking in off the street and being able to sit down in her chair and have their tattoo. If they couldn't wait for the next available appointment, usually six weeks later, then she would send them to Thumper; he had a few tattooists so could usually accommodate them.

But now she was closing for two weeks, at least on weekdays. She had a couple of bookings for the weekend in between, but the Jury Service was going to create a huge hole in her finances. She had read all the literature about expenses and had even made a few phone calls: yes, they would pay her expenses but proving how much she would lose in business was going to be difficult to do. It didn't seem a very fair system; if you were employed your employer had a duty to pay your wages. It was another let-down by the government for using your noggin' and wanting to make a better life for yourself.

It was done though. She had plenty of bookings for when she returned from Court and she would try and keep on top of any telephone messages. It was more anyone calling in off-spec that she was worried about. But she had made a notice to put on the door and she hoped that they would either ring, or send her a message on Facebook.

The rest of the day flew by. Another two tattoos completed, she was happy with all the ones she had done that day; they had all turned out beautifully. In the little backroom that was her kitchen-cum-office, she sent off a couple of emails and then cashed up her takings for the day. Hopefully she would get a chance to get to the bank when she got away from Court the next day. Satisfied that everything was cleaned up, switched off and she had everything she needed until she got back to the shop, she locked up and made her way home.

The following morning saw Lola all suited and booted; her usually wild hair was tied up in a ponytail and she had removed some of the piercings, especially the ones in her eyebrow, nose and lip. She didn't really know why she was dressing as she was, she didn't know what to expect, but thought at least on the first day she should turn up looking a little more like a decent human being and less of the delinquent look she preferred.

Following the instructions she had received with her summons, she made her way through the security procedures at the Crown Court, showing the identification documents she had been asked to bring over and over again. Then she and her fellow Jury Service members were taken into a holding area where there was a café and lots of seating areas. Half an hour later the place was packed. There were new jurors like herself, but there were others who seemed to know each other quite well; she assumed that these were either there for their second week or they were already sitting in Courts and the trial had gone on longer than the two weeks that they had been originally summoned to sit.

Lola hadn't thought about trials going on longer. Of course they did, she had seen them on television all of the time, especially murder trials where they went on for months and months. She prayed that she wasn't given a big case. A woman came in wearing a long black cloak and asked all new jurors to follow her. They were ushered into a court and for the next hour they were given advice and instruction about what was expected of each and every one of them. Back in the café, the newbies all sat together drinking their hot drinks and talking about what they had been told. It all seemed like a very daunting prospect. They all agreed though, on the up side, they all now had vouchers to redeem at the café, which no doubt wouldn't last as long as the week did, the prices were just so expensive.

And then they sat. And they sat. By the time lunch time arrived she felt like she had known all these people for years. It felt like it did when you were on holiday and quickly made strong friendships with other holidaymakers. It was all a bit surreal. Lunchtime came and went; she did think about going out and trying to find a bank, but no one else seemed to be leaving so she continued to sit. There were televisions everywhere, all turned down low so if you wanted to watch it you had to go and sit up close and personal with it. There were puzzles and books, soft chairs, hard chairs. It was clear that lots of people did lots of sitting in this area.

From time to time the ushers would come in wearing their long black cloaks, call out names, and when your name was called you had to follow the usher to wherever it was they took the jurors to. By 2pm her name still hadn't been called. Other newbies had gone, a couple had even come back to continue sitting. They had tales about not being selected because they knew the defendant or a solicitor or they knew of the case so wouldn't be able to hear the case subjectively. It was all very correct.

Lola was just about giving up hope when another usher swept in with clipboard in hand. The name calling began and then she heard it, Lorraine Harrison. She picked up her belongings and scuttled across to the doorway where the usher was waiting for them all. 'Lorraine!' There was only her mam called her that these days, everyone else called her Lola; she didn't even think that many would even know that she had been Lorraine before she went to university and renamed herself after the showgirl, at that time she couldn't have been as far removed from looking like a show girl if she tried. More like a witch!

They all followed the usher through corridors, up

lifts, down little stairwells until they eventually stood outside Court Number 3. Now it was happening and it was real, she was terrified. What lay beyond the doors? What if it was a child abuser or a rapist? Would she be able to give them a fair hearing? She didn't know! And then the doors were opening and they were being ushered inside by the usher! It was one of the most terrifying things she had done in her whole life.

She had expected the courtroom to be empty, but already it was packed full of barristers and solicitors, the Judge, the press and even the public gallery was packed. She took it that the two young men standing behind the glass partition were the defendants. Next came the Oath; she didn't think she was a nervous person, but standing up and reading off the card with all of those people watching her was horrific. It seemed to take an age to be her turn and all the time she could feel her legs turning to jelly. And then it was over and she could relax.

Someone was talking, she wasn't sure what it was about. She was trying really hard to concentrate but kept looking at the defendants. Were they rapists? Child abusers? Armed robbers? She really did need to concentrate and then she might find out. Yes, she understood that part, they were making opening statements and then they were going to adjourn for the day. Oh, they were drug dealers! How did she feel about that? She wasn't sure; she had been to university and on the club scene years ago, there were drugs everywhere and of course she had had a dabble. But the people behind the drugs, the ones that made the money…

The two lads standing in the dock didn't look like drug barons, they looked like any other young lad that had come into Thunder's shop. But not the prosecutor. How quick she had picked up the legal system, she thought to herself. The prosecutor was saying that the two defendants were just two very small fish; sprats, he had called them. But catching them would cause the bigger fish to at least have concerns, not to mention the financial loss the people higher up the food chain would have to endure. They had been caught driving a car with cocaine stashed in the vehicle with a street value of over £100k. She was in the wrong business, she thought to herself.

She looked at the two young lads standing in the dock. Adam Mitchell and Dane Pearson. They certainly didn't look like they had made a fortune from drugs. The prosecutor was right; they were sprats, but surely the reason they had done it in the first place was for money. Love of money really was the root of all evil, she thought! They were both pleading not guilty which puzzled her. Hadn't the drugs been found in the car they were driving? Or had they not known the drugs were there? For some reason she was now looking forward to the next few days; it wasn't a rape or child abuse case; she could cope with drugs.

Having been in her own world for a few minutes, she was startled when all her fellow jurors stood up and were marched out of court. That was it for the day and they were all told that they had to return the following morning to the café they had spent most of their day in – no wonder they give everyone vouchers for the café, otherwise they would all spend a fortune on teas and coffees.

It wasn't even 4pm when she walked out of the Courts. She still had time to go and find a bank and maybe even have a little look around the shops for half an hour, it wasn't often she had chance to do what she wanted. The boys both needed new coats so she might see if she could go and get them and maybe pick up something nice for tea. She would be home in plenty of time to have tea almost ready for Anthony and the boys coming in at 6.30pm.

With a spring in her step she headed to the area of the city where she thought there was a branch of her bank. She hadn't thought about it but for the majority of the day her takings had been in her handbag and her handbag had been in a locker in the cloakroom. She laughed to herself. Surely there wouldn't be any criminals in the Courts?? The queue was huge in the bank, something that usually had her nerves on edge, but today she had plenty of time. She shuffled along behind her fellow bankers and dug into her handbag for the paying-in book.

Not a bad week's work, she thought to herself, glancing at the paying-in slip. £857, that wasn't including the money she had taken in card payments. Tats for Tarts really was turning out to be much better than she could have hoped for. Hard work, yes, but wasn't anything that was worth doing? She handed over her book and cash. It included £10, HE75 229564. Thanking the teller she made her way out of the bank and off towards Fenwick's which she hoped would have the coats in that the boys had been badgering her about. At almost £100 each she thought it was daylight robbery. Money wasn't everything, but it certainly helped.

Mark 12:41-44

And he sat down opposite the treasury and watched the people putting money into the offering box. Many rich people put in large sums. And a poor widow came and put in two small copper coins, which make a penny. And he called his disciples to him and said to them, "Truly, I say to you, this poor widow has put in more than all those who are contributing to the offering box. For they all contributed out of their abundance, but she out of her poverty has put in everything she had, all she had to live on."

ABOUT THE AUTHOR

My name is Gill Burnett. I live in the North East.

I do not come from a literary background, but I have lived. I watch people and I listen.

A few years ago I started to write and I can hand on heart say I love it. I have a handful of stories waiting to come out. But like many I have a day job so writing is for spare time and holidays.

I love the characters I create; even the more dubious ones. I hope you love them all too because I have so much more to give. Hopefully *Take Note!* is just the beginning of me and you!

Printed in Poland
by Amazon Fulfillment
Poland Sp. z o.o., Wrocław

53799254R00152